MURDER AT BAYFIELD RIVER

A ROSE BLAIR MURDER MYSTERY

JUDY KEIGHTLEY

COZY HOUSE PRESS

COZY HOUSE PRESS
MAKE A DATE WITH MURDER

An Imprint for GracePoint Publishing (www.GracePointPublishing.com)

GracePoint Matrix, LLC
624 S. Cascade Ave
Suite 201
Colorado Springs, CO 80903
www.GracePointMatrix.com
Email: Admin@GracePointMatrix.com
SAN # 991-6032

ISBN-13: (Paperback) –978-1-951694-48-7
eISBN: (eBook) - 978-1-951694-47-0

Books may be purchased for educational, business, or sales promotional use.
For bulk order requests and price schedule contact:
Orders@GracePointPublishing.com

MAKE A DATE WITH MURDER...

Find Cozy House Press online to read more great cozy mysteries!

www.cozyhousepress.com

COZY HOUSE PRESS

MAKE A DATE WITH MURDER

This novel is dedicated to our beautiful Nova Scotian Duck Toller, Lucy, who died too soon at the age of seven. She is terribly missed by all. R.I.P. darling princess. I would also like to dedicate this book to my always supportive husband and family and to all those that tirelessly work to protect our environment and who are the inspiration for this novel.

ONE

Ryan stood at the edge of the approach to the new bridge over the Bayfield River surveying the scene before him. The temporary bypass bridge was in and opened, the old bridge had been demolished and the beginnings of the two large concrete abutments were rising up majestically from each side of the river, bearing the heavy cages of reinforced metal bars which seemed to poke incongruously out of the top of the shutters. The new bridge was beginning to take shape. After months of waiting for the contract to be awarded Ryan was pleased that they were now on schedule and making rapid progress on the planned two-year project.

He looked at his watch. It was only seven o'clock, his best time of the day. The rest of the construction team would be arriving soon, but Ryan always made it a point of arriving half an hour earlier. He liked to start his day peacefully, to enjoy his cup of coffee that he had picked up from Shop Bike on the main street in the village, to light up a cigarette, the one and only of the day, and to give himself time to reflect on the world and the day ahead.

Ryan walked over to the metal safety fence which also overlooked the river flats. There wasn't a single fisherman out on the river that morning, which was quite unusual, until he remembered that there had been a fishing derby just the previous weekend and those same fishermen were probably now enjoying a break from catching fish.

Ryan looked down to where the river meandered and flowed over white rocks and around what looked like an island which spawned tall grasses and a few spindly trees. He could see a deeper channel of water barely twenty feet across where he supposed one could navigate a small boat.

The river looked particularly fresh and sparkling that day with the early morning sun already casting bright rays across the twinkling water. Ryan surveyed the riverbank and then looked back again at what appeared to be a pile of clothing, or maybe some garbage, stuck in the long grasses by the side of the riverbank and close to the actual bridge construction. He glanced at his watch again. There was still fifteen minutes left of his precious peace, time enough to go and investigate the mound of clothing or whatever it was that had caught his attention from above.

Ryan walked back up the hill until he came to the entrance to the river flats. This piece of land, so he had been told, had been purchased by the community and put into trust to be used by the public and to be maintained as natural habitat. There was a small car park at the bottom of the steep hill by the edge of the embankment where the new bridge abutments were taking shape. Ryan walked to the river's edge and looked along the bank trying to find what he had spied from above. Scanning the bank, he suddenly noticed the change in the ebb and flow of the water. He walked towards the unnatural flow and peered down through the tangled mass of reeds and branches. There, barely visible to the naked eye, he could see a leg twisted around a floating log. His eyes followed the limb and realization clicked in that he was looking at the body of a man half submerged in the swirling water channelling around the body like the ebbing tide of a seaside beach.

Ryan pulled out his phone, and feeling strangely detached from the situation, tapped in 911. Later, when asked, he would say that it had all seemed unreal to him finding the body of a man trapped amongst the flotsam of the Bayfield River, and that he had no recollection of even making the phone call to the police. When further asked how he knew that the man was actually dead, Ryan could only say that he just knew without turning the body over, that there was absolutely no life left in the poor soul and that it was pretty obvious that the back of the man's head had been bashed to a pulp.

TWO

Rose and Susan sat out on the patio enjoying the beautiful June morning. For a moment Rose experienced a twinge of guilt as Friday was when she usually went to her fitness class, but Susan had telephoned suggesting that they met for coffee and, oh well, her arm had been twisted. Now here they were, enjoying coffee under the umbrella, and listening to the cardinals sing out their plaintive songs while Ben and Puff gently snored under the patio table.

"Listen to your dogs, Rose, I've never heard such a racket, do they always snore like this?" Susan said laughingly, her eyes twinkling, and her sensuous mouth curved up in a beguiling smile.

"Yes, they both snore like troopers and at night you can add Tom to the mix too. Now, Susan, have another scone, I made them especially for you."

Susan helped herself to another orange and cranberry scone and smothered it with a generous pat of butter. Rose watched as her friend scoffed the lot down and marvelled just how much she ate yet still maintained her lovely slim body.

"So, have you heard anything from Tone? When is he due back in Bayfield?"

Susan's face clouded over at the mention of Tone. It had been almost a year since she had left Italy and her husband behind. He had promised to sort out his drug and gambling problem yet, so far, he had not returned to Canada. Susan had received several letters full of empty promises, but so far, he had not delivered the goods. She let out a deep sigh and looked at her friend with wide, sorrowful eyes.

"I don't think that he'll ever come back here to Bayfield, Rose. Living in Elba and mixing with the jet set the way he did has just given him too much of a taste for the high life. All the vices he had worked so hard in the police force to stamp out seem to have engulfed Tone. I'm convinced he'll never be able to break away because the simple truth is that he is intoxicated with it all."

Susan's eyes began to well up with tears. Rose got up and put her arms around her friend.

"I'm so sorry, Susan, so very sorry. Now dry your eyes. I've got a surprise for you."

Rose disappeared into the house and returned holding a white, fluffy bundle. She handed the tiny kitten over to her friend saying, "My sister's cat Riley had kittens and this little darling is the last of the litter. I thought that you might like to adopt her. She's about six weeks old and Kate was going to keep both of the kittens, but I asked her if I could give this beauty to you."

Susan stroked the kitten and then held it up to her face and smiled. "You know something Rose, she's perfect and thank you. I'll have to think of a name for her."

Just then Tom came rushing in. Rose could see by his face

that he had some news as he barged onto the patio calling out her name.

"Rose, Rose, you'll never guess what. That DCI Hargreaves is down by the river flats. Apparently, there's been another possible murder. A construction worker found the body. Oh, hello Susan, I didn't see you. Sorry for interrupting, I just knew that Rose would be interested. Umm...I'll go inside now."

Rose smiled and said, "Calm down Tom, come and join us for coffee. Look, I've given Susan Muffy, so that's one less thing for you to worry about."

Tom had been complaining about allergies as he swore that the kitten made his eyes water and itch, and that he was concerned about Puff and Ben ganging up on the little thing. *On a whole, Tom had turned into a big fuss pot,* Rose thought and wondered if the heart attack he had suffered the previous year had contributed to his general anxiety, or maybe it was just another aspect of his getting older. She looked at her husband affectionately though and mused that he looked pretty good after losing some weight and keeping to his fitness regime. Tom had in fact been out pole walking with a group of men who twice a week walked five kilometres around the village. Also, the golf season had started in earnest. Yes, her husband was on a good fitness routine and hopefully he would manage to keep it up.

Susan smiled at Tom and their eyes engaged momentarily and just for a second, Rose felt her own heart catch. She had seen that look before and had always known that Tom was attracted to her friend, but this time, the look made Rose hold her breath.

"Umm...Tom, would you like a scone?" she said handing

the plate over to him. Tom took a scone and pulled up a chair to join Rose and Susan.

"So, you were saying that you saw D.C.I. Hargreaves down at the river flats. Did you speak to him?"

Rose had not seen John Hargreaves for almost a year. Memories of the handsome, six foot four, black detective came flooding back to her as she recalled the previous summer when she had got to know him quite well. John had been investigating the murder at Windmill Lake.

Rose visibly blushed just thinking about the chemistry that had clearly sparked between them which had ultimately led to a passionate kiss. This still made Rose feel warm and fuzzy all over just at the mere thought, but that was a year ago and life had gone on despite the sense of betrayal Rose had felt at the time.

"No, I didn't get to talk to him, but I saw him with Constables Brown and Elliot. They were cordoning off the River Flats with yellow tape. The ambulance was there, and I even noticed that doctor's car, what's his name, the one that lives on the farm down Porters Line?"

Susan's eyes lit up. "You mean Doctor Green, the pathologist from Goderich?"

"Yes, that's him. You know he came out to one of my Rotary meetings a couple of months ago and gave us a really interesting talk on pathology. I like the chap."

It had been a couple of years since Susan had worked with Doctor Green. At one stage she had the distinct feeling that he had fancied her then, that was of course before she had met Tone and it now felt like a million years ago.

"Oh, Tom, I wonder if one of the construction workers got injured, but that wouldn't warrant a visit from DCI Hargreaves, would it?"

Rose felt anxious on several levels, not the least of which was the possibility of seeing John again and what old feelings might resurface.

"Well, love, we'll soon find out I'm sure, you know what the village is like. No news is good news. Now I'm off to play golf so I'll see you after lunch." Tom gave Rose a quick kiss and proceeded to leave.

"Tom's looking good, Rose. He seems to have regained his energy and I also notice that he's lost some weight." Susan said whilst buttering another scone.

Rose still felt distracted, she nodded her head and smiled at Susan. "Yes, it's been quite a relief for me, you know; although it's been hard keeping Tom from eating scones and bread. I know that I've made these today, but now I only bake if we are having guests. I've also cut down on our meat and potatoes by almost half. Mind you, it's a bit frustrating seeing as how Tom's lost thirty pounds and I've barely lost five!"

The phone rang just as Rose was about to make another pot of coffee. It was DCI John Hargreaves. Rose's heart gave a lurch as she listened to his deep voice.

"Rose, this is John. Look, I'm in the village investigating a murder and I'd love to catch up with you. Would it be alright if I called by in say forty minutes time?"

Rose looked at her watch. It was only eleven, Tom would be playing golf until at least two and Susan would be leaving soon.

"Umm...yes, that would be lovely." She said and put the phone down.

"I'll just make some more coffee, if you'd like it," Rose said but Susan stood up and shook her head.

"I'm coffee'd out, Rose. No, I must be on my way, I'll have

to go to the pet shop in Goderich to pick up some kitten food, a bed, and some cat litter."

Susan gave Rose a quick hug and walked around the side of the house. "I'll show myself out, Rose, bye."

"Oh, Susan," Rose called after her friend, "Take some of these scones with you. Tom will only eat them if they're left. I'll just pop into the kitchen and get a paper bag for them."

THREE

After Susan had gone, Rose was left alone with her thoughts. Hearing John's voice again had stirred up all the dormant, pent-up emotions that she had buried inside her and it made her feel decidedly unsettled. *Pull yourself together*, Rose admonished herself and got busy washing up the coffee cups and tidying the kitchen while deliberately blanking out the nervous anticipation she was experiencing.

The doorbell rang and Rose jumped. She walked to the door her mouth feeling dry and her stomach fluttering. Opening the door, she immediately took in the handsome figure of DCI Hargreaves just standing there with a daft expression on his face.

"Umm...John, come in. How lovely to see you."

John stepped inside and Rose closed the door. Almost immediately she found herself embraced in his strong arms and before she could say anything, he was kissing her, and her body was responding in a way she could not stop. Rose found herself drowning in John's passionate kiss and she longed for more. She bent her body into his and he pulled her tightly and ran his hands hungrily over her breasts which were now straining against the fabric of her t-shirt. His fingers squeezed her nipples and she let out a low groan. Still not a single word had been spoken. John began to pull her t-shirt over her head and Rose tugged at his pants. Both were panting and oblivious to the world. John ran his hands into her pants and held her bottom tightly. She could feel his manhood throbbing and she wanted him so badly that she found herself wrapping her legs around his and thrusting her pelvis forward as she let out another groan and managed to whisper, "Take me, John, take me."

Suddenly, just as Rose was wriggling out of her clothing and panting as if in labour, the telephone rang and it was then, and only then, that reason and sensibility broke through and reality hit her with a bang.

"Oh my God, John, what are we doing? Oh my, oh my, this is so wrong."

Rose pushed away from him and ran to the kitchen where she picked up the phone.

"Oh, Rose, it's Kate. Look, I'm at Food Basics and wondered if there was anything you needed me to get for you?"

"Umm... well, I can't think right now, do you mind if I call you back in five minutes?"

"No problem, are you sure that you're okay? You sound a bit weird."

"I'm fine, I ran to get to the phone so I suppose I could be a bit out of breath. I'll speak to you soon."

Rose put the phone down and turned to face John who

had pulled up his pants while she straightened up her clothing and ran her fingers through her messed up hair. They looked at each other for what seemed like forever before Rose sighed and finally said, "John, I don't know what just happened, but I do know that it cannot happen again. Look, I love Tom. I'm a happily married woman and I cannot let this thing between us go any further. Oh God, I'm so attracted to you, but I also know that it's wrong and I cannot, and I will not, be unfaithful to Tom, so we're going to pretend that this never happened, right?"

John nodded, but at the same time his eyes were pleading to Rose. He finally spoke softly taking her hands in his. "Rose, my darling, I will respect your wishes, of course I will, but please promise me that should you change your mind about Tom that I'll be the first to know because, you see, I love you and it breaks my heart that I can't have you."

He squeezed her hands and let them go, coughed, and then in a brusquer voice he continued. "Now I actually do have a problem that maybe you can help me with. It looks like the body found in the river flats is a murder victim and as such I will have to lead the investigation. Last year I managed to secure The Lion's Hall but right now it is being renovated so we can't use it as our incident room. Do you know of another venue that we could adopt for our incident room?"

Rose thought for a minute and then said. "The basement of the Town hall could be an option. Do you want me to show you the space? We have several weddings booked, but other than the kitchen, the rest of the basement is rarely used. What do you think?"

A couple of years previously, Rose had joined the town hall committee and was now their chairperson. She had found the position extremely demanding and a lot of hard work, but she had told the committee that she would give them two years and then they would have to look for another chair.

"I think that you're a genius and yes, let's go and take a look right now. Do you want to come in my car or take your own?"

Rose thought about it and then said, "I can only be ten minutes as I'm supposed to be calling Kate back. Look, I'll take my car so that if you decide to take the space, I can leave you there and you can start setting up."

With that settled, Rose called Puff and Ben inside and followed John out to the front drive where her old Volvo sat next to his black Jaguar.

"Hey, that's a new car, John, isn't it?"

"Yes, isn't she a beauty. It's a Jaguar I-Pace, all electric SUV."

"Wow, you obviously love your cars."

Rose got into her beat up old Volvo, reversed, and John followed behind. They drove down Bayfield Terrace to Louisa Street and then drove around Clan Gregor Square to the town hall. Rose got out and punched in the door code.

"Look, John, I'll give you the door code if you decide to use the basement; now there will be a rental fee, but it won't be much."

John nodded and followed Rose into the small lobby. Immediately in front of them was a short, steep flight of stairs and to the left another flight of stairs that led to the basement. He continued to follow Rose as she walked down the stairs and past the kitchen; he practically walked into the back of her when she abruptly stopped and pointed to a small room to the right.

"That's the Town Hall jail. Five years ago, Joe Berry of

The Berries was found murdered with a kitchen knife stabbed through his neck." Rose shuddered at the memory.

"And I suppose you were involved, Rose?" John had come up close behind her and began to run his hand down her spine; she whipped around and pushed his hand away.

"John, what did you not understand about me saying we can't do this? Every time that you come near me like this you send shivers down my spine. Do you think that I like rejecting you? I want you as much as you desire me, but we're not children, we're adults and we don't always get what we want. Now, come and see this room before I give in and become another statistic on the adultery scale."

John laughed and went into the basement room letting out a low whistle. "This is perfect, Rose, thank you, as long as we can get wi-fi I can proceed with setting everything up. Can I say thank you with a kiss?"

"No, John, no more kisses. Right, I'll leave you now to your investigation. Here's the door code, I've written it down for you. By the way, do you know who the dead man is?"

"No, all we know is that he's an older guy, probably in his sixties, grey hair, and average height. He was wearing casual clothes, a blue plaid shirt and jeans. We'll know more after forensics have finished and the pathologist has worked his magic."

Rose walked to the stairs and turned to John.

"Let me know if you need anything else. I'll invite you around for dinner, but you have to promise to behave. No touching me or, for that matter, coming physically near to me."

John smiled and put out his hands in mock surrender. "It's a deal, Mrs. Blair. Anything to sample your cooking. Now you had better go before I break all my promises and ravage you right here and now."

His eyes twinkled and he laughed in such a way that Rose had to steel herself to leave. She so wanted to succumb to him in every way possible. Gulping a deep breath of air, she faintly said "Bye, John. Good luck with the investigation."

Turning her back on John, Rose walked out of the Town Hall wiping the welling tears from her eyes.

FOUR

K ate arrived at Rose and Tom's house only to find the driveway empty. She was greeted by a cacophony of barking dogs with Ben and Puff looking at her from the other side of the glass door.

Kate tried the handle; it was unlocked as usual. After a boisterous greeting from both the dogs she went into the kitchen and put the kettle on. Wherever her sister had gone she was fairly confident that she would be back soon. Rose, if nothing else, had always been reliable and had, indeed, been her rock, her saviour, particularly when her ex-husband had run off with her best friend.

It had been Rose who had invited Kate to stay with them in Bayfield and had encouraged her to make the move from Kelowna in British Columbia to the village. She had helped her to establish herself, to heal and to regain some self-esteem. So much so that she was now working at the Albion three days a week plus helping out at the animal rescue in Stratford. She adored her little cottage on Louisa Street, and she absolutely loved Rose and Tom with a passion.

Kate had just made a pot of tea and had carried the tray into the sunroom when she heard Rose come in through the front door.

"Rose, I'm through here in the sunroom with the dogs, I hope you don't mind, but I've made some tea."

At the sound of her sister's voice Rose smiled and went to join her in the sunroom. The minute that Kate looked at her she said, "Rose, are you alright? You look kind of strange."

"Oh, don't mind me, I've just been rushing around like a mad thing. Now, what about you? Oh, I gave that darling kitten to Susan this morning and she loved him. How is your kitten doing?"

"He's great although I think that Riley is thoroughly exhausted. All he does is run around and jump on his poor mother and pounce on anything moving: like my feet, first thing in the morning. Honestly, he's a riot, but changing the subject somewhat, there's something going on at the bridge, Rose. There is yellow tape by the entrance to the river flats and police cars and loads of activity going on down by the river, do you know what's up?"

Rose smiled, "Yes, I'll tell you all I know, which isn't much. I'm afraid to say that there's been another murder in the village. Pour out the tea and I'll tell you what little I know."

FIVE

By the time the team had been assembled John had already been in contact with the Emergency Response Team known as ERT, and the IDENT team. No decision had yet been made on whether the services of USRU, the Underwater Search and Recovery Unit, based in Toronto would be required. That would depend on the results of the forensic examination. Doctor Green, the pathologist, had conducted his medical examination and the body had been removed to the Goderich mortuary. John felt confident that for the time being he had covered all the bases.

Sergeant Flowers and Constable Brown arrived first and shook hands with John.

"It's good to see you again." Sergeant Flowers said and John smiled. He had really enjoyed working with his team the previous year and had high expectations for the upcoming investigation.

Constable Holly Ryan and Constable Elliot arrived just as the others had taken their seats.

"This is cosy," Holly said as she looked around the room, "No computers though?"

"The incident board, computers and all the other paraphernalia is being trucked down from HQ in London. They should all be here hopefully by this afternoon. Right, everyone, welcome to the Town Hall, now, let's get started; Constable Ryan, could you be our scribe?"

Holly nodded and took out her tablet as John started.

"No need for introductions, but may I say how pleased I am to have you all back here with me again. Let's hope that we can have this murder solved within the next forty-eight hours as it should be a relatively easy one to put together.

"So, let's look at what we know. Ryan Woods, a bridge construction worker, found the body at 7:20 this morning. It lay tangled in the reeds on the banks of the Bayfield River with one leg wedged around a tree branch and the whole torso partially submerged in about one foot of water. The legs were pointing downstream as if the body had floated in that direction before getting stuck in the riverbank and the man's head had been bashed to a pulp.

"So far, no identification has been found on the body. IDENT is on to it, forensics and the SOC team have taken photographs, fingerprints will be taken, teeth x-rayed, and DNA sampled. Hopefully all of that will have been done by now by our resident pathologist, Doctor Green. It appears now to be just a waiting game, waiting for all the results to come in. Any questions?"

Constable Ryan put up her hand.

"Yes, Holly."

"What makes you think that he was murdered and that it wasn't just an accident?"

"Good question, and my fault for not including the fact that our John Doe had the back of his skull smashed in."

"Could he not have hit his head against a rock or something when falling into the river?" Holly persisted.

"Not with the severity of the damage inflicted. We will know more after the autopsy, but no, we are definitely dealing with a murder."

Sergeant Flowers put up his hand. "So, we have no idea who this man is and what he was doing in the river?"

John nodded and said with a slightly impatient voice, "The ERT will be scouring the river for clues as to where the man went into the water and, of course, they will be looking for the murder weapon which is probably a stick or a bat or something of that ilk.

"Waiting, my friends, is a hard pill to swallow, but in the meantime, we can be asking the public if they know of a man in his fifties or sixties who has gone missing in the last twelve hours. To that end, I would like Constables Brown and Elliot to ask around the marina and the village to see if anyone might recognize our John Doe.

"Sergeant Flowers I want you to liaise with the ERT. I will be contacting Doctor Green who has scheduled the autopsy for this afternoon at 3:00 p.m. which I will attend. Today we'll have an easy start, but tomorrow we'll be back to meeting both morning and afternoon. So, go to it team and see you all tomorrow."

The officers gathered up their notepads and Constable Ryan finished typing up and distributing the minutes of their first team meeting. As the rest of them filed out of the basement Holly approached John.

"Sir, I wanted to let you know that I'm getting married in a couple of weeks. It won't affect this case, well, hopefully we won't be working on the day of my wedding, I just thought that I'd let you know."

John smiled broadly and put out his hand to congratulate his young officer.

"Well, done, Holly, I truly hope that you'll be very happy together indeed. Do I know the lucky man?"

"I doubt it. His name is Gary, and he works for the municipality." Holly laughed and said that she was feeling nervous as she hated to be the centre of attention.

"Well you can't escape that if you choose to have a big wedding." John said with a smile remembering his own daughter Rachel's wedding five years ago when his darling wife Mary was still with them, and just how beautiful both mother and daughter had looked on that very special day.

"Oh, but we're not having a big wedding, sir, just my family and Gary's parents, about ten of us in total. We're having the reception at Thyme on 21 in Goderich."

"Oh well, that won't be so bad for you. You'll probably enjoy the day. Where are you actually getting married?"

"Oh, on a boat. We're being married by the captain in the middle of Lake Huron."

John must have looked quite surprised as Holly continued to say, "Oh, sir, don't look so aghast. We wanted a different kind of wedding and Gary loves to sail so that's why we chose to be married on a boat."

"Well, I have to say that's certainly different. Right, I must lock up and head over to Goderich. The autopsy is at three o'clock and I haven't yet checked in to The Little Inn, let alone had any lunch."

Holly walked up the stairs and out into the blazing sunlight followed by DCI Hargreaves who diligently locked the town hall door behind him.

SIX

After Kate left, Rose went into top gear cleaning the kitchen, then deciding to take the dogs for a quick walk before heading out to the croquet courts where she was meeting her friend Lynda. They both had foolishly signed up for a tournament and now were obligated to play five games. Rose had fortunately been paired up with Lynda and they were to play Ed and Jerry in the first game.

Walking down Bayfield Terrace with Puff pulling and Ben stopping every two minutes to sniff at some delectable smell, Rose pulled at their leashes and paused in front of Hannah and Allan's house wondering how Allan was doing.

Last time she had spoken to Hannah, Allan was undergoing chemotherapy and had not been responding at all well to the treatment. He had been diagnosed with a form of leukaemia several months ago and it had come as a big shock as Allan had always been a picture of good health.

It was not just Allan who had fallen ill, Rose thought, as she continued her walk, other friends, mostly men and husbands of her friends, had also fallen ill. *We're all getting old*, she thought as she reached Pioneer Park.

Walking down the steps to the beach, Rose remembered the previous summer when there had been no sand at all as the lake levels had risen so high as to envelope the whole space that used to be a lovely public beach. This year the lake levels had dropped and thankfully a small beach area had been recovered, enough for Puff and Ben to frolic along. Rose picked up a stick and threw it into the lake. Ben ran after it and charged into the water followed by a less enthusiastic Puff.

Looking out across the azure blue lake Rose could see several sail boats gliding across the water. It reminded her that *Tranquillity*, their sailing boat needed a good clean as Paul, Atsuko, and baby Yuki had visited them the previous weekend and had taken the boat out for a long sail. Tom had accompanied them leaving Rose to baby sit Yuki. She had made them a picnic lunch to have on board and they had left the food containers on the boat. *Tom and I should go for a sail this evening,* Rose thought before she remembered that Tom had a Rotary meeting. It seemed to be that they rarely had time to sail their boat these days.

Calling the dogs in from the lake Rose clipped their leashes back on and proceeded to walk back up Long Hill Road. She could see as far as the bridge construction and wondered quite what was going on and then she couldn't stop herself from thinking about John Hargreaves again and what had transpired between them. It fairly took her breath away just thinking about the moment of madness that had almost consumed both of them.

Reaching their house on Bayfield Terrace, Rose let the dogs in and proceeded to go to her bedroom to change into her whites ready for the croquet match. She had ten minutes to get ready and eat some lunch before driving to the courts out on David Street.

Arriving bang on time, Rose saw Lynda standing beneath one of the tented pavilions. She looked around for Jerry and Ed and saw no sign of them anywhere. Walking up to Lynda she said,

"Have you seen our partners, Lynda?"

"No. We do have the right day and time, don't we, Rose?"

"Yes, I checked the schedule pinned up in the shed and we are down to play Jerry and Ed today at two o'clock."

"Oh well, we'll give them a while longer." Lynda said and sat down on one of the benches overlooking the courts. "By the way, Rose, did you hear about the murder? A man was found by the river flats with his head beaten in. There's a whole load of men in diving suits searching the river right now. I wonder who the poor dead man is?"

Rose went quiet and then said, "Yes, I was talking to DCI Hargreaves who is investigating the murder. They have to wait for the results of the autopsy, and they might have to rely on dental records for identification as apparently nobody has a clue who the man might be."

"Well I hope they find the murderer soon; it gives me the creeps thinking about someone capable of murder being loose in Bayfield."

"I think that you would be surprised at how many people in the village would be capable of murder, Lynda."

Jerry pulled into the car park on his own without Ed.

"I wonder where Ed has gone." Lynda said as she walked towards Jerry.

"Sorry you two," Jerry said," Ed can't make it as he's not feeling well, a bit under the weather. Look, we'll re-schedule our game if that's alright by you?"

Lynda and Rose agreed to arrange another match when Ed was feeling better. *I hope that Ed is not going to join the list of other sick men in the village,* Rose thought as she got up to leave.

"Right, I'm going home to prepare a nice meal for Tom. I've been out pretty well all day on and off so I'm more than happy to stay in for the rest of the day and cook. See you soon, Lynda."

Lynda smiled and went to get in her car while Rose drove off in her old Volvo feeling quite relieved that she didn't have to play croquet after all. She felt far too preoccupied with her thoughts of John to be able to concentrate on a game.

SEVEN

D CI Hargreaves stood in the small mortuary feeling decidedly unhappy at the prospect of witnessing the autopsy. He hadn't been to one for a number of years and certainly had never attended one in Canada. Doctor Green, however seemed a decent sort and appeared very professional with his headset and microphone on to give a running commentary of the procedure.

The body was laid out on a stainless-steel gurney wheeled in by one of the technicians who proceeded to gently roll it onto the mortician's slab which had two channels each side to serve as drainage for all the body fluids.

John watched as Doctor Green picked up a scalpel and made a large Y incision on the chest of the dead man's torso. He then pulled the flaps of skin to one side and cracked open the sternum, first looking at the lungs, he then plunged his hands inside the chest cavity and pulled out the organs one by one to be weighed on scales.

Doctor Green, however, instead of weighing the organs, paused and looked intently at the liver and kidneys. John was both fascinated and repulsed by what he could see, and he wasn't sure why the doctor had stopped to study the organs so intently before weighing them and placing them back inside the body.

Finally, he pulled down his mask and spoke to John. "I'm sorry detective, but I'm going to have to send this body to Toronto to their forensics laboratory. They have a lot more sophisticated equipment and I believe this man has something seriously wrong with his organs.

"As to time of death, I would say that, based on the internal temperature of the body and allowing for the temperature of the river where it was found, death took place sometime between five and eight o'clock last night. The back of the skull has been smashed in and significant brain matter is missing. Cause of death would have been a result of trauma from a single blunt instrument shaped like a log or a baseball bat.

"As to the deceased's age, I would put him at around fifty-five to sixty. Judging from his hands I would say that he was not a labourer or farmer, his nails are clean and well-manicured, and his teeth look quite good with no crowns, dental caps or, indeed, any fillings which is quite unusual for a man of his age.

"I'm afraid that's all I can tell you right now, but I do have to say that judging from the state of this man's organs, he was one really sick man. Oh, and another thing I forgot to mention is he definitely did not drown. He was already dead before he hit the water"

"How can you tell that?" John said.

"His lungs are not filled with water." Doctor Green answered as he prepared to leave the room.

John thanked him and bade his farewells. Most of what he had been told other than the sick looking organs, he had already deduced, John thought as he left the hospital and drove back to Bayfield. He hoped that the Emergency Response Team might have some better news. They really needed to identify the man and soon.

The Underwater Search and Rescue and the ERT were still combing the river when John arrived at the river flats. He walked over to the officer in charge.

"Let's have an update, officer. Have your teams found anything significant?"

The officer shook his head and said, "The Marine Unit has just arrived from Grand Bend. They're about to take the *Zodiac* out upriver. Would you care to join them?"

John jumped at the opportunity. He hated inaction and had begun to feel that the case was going stale before it had even begun.

"Sure, I'd love to go with them. Thank you."

The *Zodiac* took off with four divers and John on board. They motored past the banks of the Sawmill Creek River Trail and continued upstream until the water became so shallow that they were about ready to turn back. Passing through another bend in the river, John pointed to an area on the river-bank where the grass had been trampled flat. He asked if they could stop and have a closer look.

As they reached the riverbank, they found themselves by a small manmade dock which had long since been overgrown and somewhat neglected with tall grasses and river reeds almost hiding the dock itself.

John climbed out of the *Zodiac* and looked around. *This could be a fisherman's hideout*, he thought as his eyes scoured the riverbank. Suddenly he saw a tiny piece of blue fabric clinging to some spindly grasses. He pointed this out to the Marine Unit and used his smart phone to take some pictures of his own before the diving unit brought out their own professional cameras and started to photograph the scene methodically.

Suddenly, one of the men shouted out excitedly and pointed to a clump of reeds. There an old log lay on the ground; it was about two foot in length with blood, gristle mixed with human hair, and bone ingrained in the bark at one end. There was absolutely no doubt that they had found the murder weapon.

With the grizzly log photographed and the crime scene secured with tape, the murder weapon was placed carefully into a sealed bag which would be sent to Toronto. Hair, blood, and DNA would be extracted, and much information gathered. This, however, would take days and possibly weeks.

Before the Marine Unit left the scene of the crime John decided to explore the immediate area surrounding the overgrown dock. Most of the riverbank was almost impassable with weeds and grasses almost to shoulder height, but John could see a defined pathway leading up the steep slope away from the river. He walked up the pathway until halfway up the bank, he noticed what looked like a large shed.

On closer inspection, he found, nestled in the dense bushes, an old cottage. The property was so overgrown that it was either abandoned or had been deliberately left in seclusion.

Leaving the small building for the time being, John continued walking up the slope until, to his surprise, he found himself in a cleared area of neat trailers sat in manicured lawns and driveways, with a proper paved road fronting the properties. He continued walking past at least twenty homes and out onto what he realized was none other than the Bayfield River Road.

He was standing at the entrance to the Happy Valley Adult Community, according to the large sign erected at the entry to the park. It was located just down the road from Windmill Lake.

John turned around and walked back the way he had come, and just in time too, as the diving team were all ready to depart. He decided he would return later to look more closely at the small cottage hidden in the bushes.

EIGHT

The smell of onions cooking greeted Tom as he walked into the house later that afternoon. Rose was busy making a chicken casserole for their dinner. Puff and Ben sat in the middle of the kitchen floor watching her intently as she chopped up the chicken pieces. Occasionally Rose threw the odd bit of meat over to the dogs always making sure that they both got a piece. An open bottle of wine sat on the counter with a glass beside it.

Rose noticed Tom eyeing the wine and she laughed saying, "This wine is for the casserole although the cook does have certain privileges."

Tom walked to Rose stepping over the dogs and gave her a kiss. "I'm meeting a few of the guys at The Black Dog at four o'clock. What time do you want me home for dinner?"

Rose smiled at Tom as she said, "Oh, we'll eat at about six. By the way, did you have a good game of golf?"

"Yes, okay, but Bill couldn't make it as he wasn't feeling well."

"That's strange as Lynda and I couldn't play our croquet

game today because Ed wasn't feeling well either. I hope that there's not a bug going around." Rose said as she went back to her cooking.

Tom wandered off to the sunroom to read the paper. He would be leaving in half an hour to join the men at The Black Dog. Rose poured half the bottle of wine into the casserole, added a generous pinch of sage, and covered the dish with a lid and placed it in the oven. She was about to start preparing the potatoes when the phone rang. It was Anne, their youngest daughter.

"Hi, Mom. How are you and Dad? I haven't heard from you for ages."

Anne always sounded upbeat and positive. Rose could just visualize their daughter with her long blond hair up in a knot, lightly freckled cheek bones, and sparkling blue eyes. She had appeared so much happier since their move from Halifax to Toronto, particularly as she had landed a tenured position as head of media studies at Ryerson.

Fortunately, her husband Allan, who had held a top job as head of the astrophysics department at Dalhousie University in Halifax, had been eligible to take early retirement and become a stay-at-home dad so that Anne could pursue her own career.

Their two children, Oliver, and Amelia, whilst being as cute as buttons, were very active and, if Rose was honest, acted like wild animals. Allan had his time cut out for him and a small part of her felt somewhat sorry for him.

"Oh, it's lovely to hear from you, dear. Dad and I are absolutely fine. Your father is doing really well, keeping fit and healthy, and still losing weight. When are you all coming to see us?"

"Well, that's one of the reasons why I'm calling." Anne

said. "My summer students are finishing their courses next week, and I thought that we could maybe come to visit you at the end of that week if that's okay?"

Rose mentally flicked through her diary. The only thing pending was the croquet tournament; she could pop out anytime for that and leave Anne and Allan with the kids. Rose knew that Tom and she would be expected to babysit for a large chunk of their visit.

"That would be great, darling. How are Oliver and Amelia and how is Allan?"

"Mom, you're doing it again, I can tell it by the tone of your voice that you feel sorry for Allan. Look, I stayed at home with the kids for two years and you didn't feel sorry for me, did you, so what's this about Allan?"

Anne was beginning to sound more like Jessica, Tom and Rose's eldest daughter who had always been feisty and direct.

"Oh, I'm sorry dear, it's just that I could never have left your father in charge of you girls and Paul. He would have been hopeless and would have never managed."

"Well, we're a different generation now, Mom, and men are supposed to pull their weight."

"Yes, I know that darling and it truly is great that men are stepping up. Look, just ignore me, I'm just old-fashioned."

Tom appeared just then, and Rose deliberately handed the phone to him mouthing that it was Anne.

"Oh, hello, love, how are you?"

Rose left Tom chatting easily to Anne while she went and poured herself a large glass of wine. Sometimes talking to their children really stressed Rose out.

She went back to peeling the potatoes and cutting up some Brussel sprouts. She would make her and Tom's favourite vegetable recipe: Brussel sprouts cooked in apple sauce, apple juice, and onions. Looking at her watch she saw that it was already four-fifteen. Tom was supposed to be meeting his mates at The Black Dog.

She went over to him and pointed to her watch and then mimed drinking a pint; Tom looked at her blankly and then understanding clicked in.

"Anne, love, I must dash. Your mother and I look forward to seeing you all next week. Love you."

Tom put the phone down, gave Rose a quick kiss on her nose, and then dashed out the door leaving Rose to her thoughts reflecting on the day's events, particularly her feelings about John.

NINE

At the Black Dog Tom's drinking buddies were all sitting together around a line of tables that had been pushed together. Mike, Ian, Wayne, and George who had originally founded the Thirsty Thursday Club were already there and had ordered a couple of pitchers of beer which now sat on the tables.

Tom glanced over to the bar and noticed DCI Hargreaves hunched over a pint. He went over and invited him to join their group. Soon the men were talking and laughing amongst each other, and the talk only turned serious when they asked John about the progress of the murder inquiry.

"So, any clues as to whom the mystery man is?" Mike asked.

John took a long swig of beer and gulped it down before answering. "Well, we're getting a little closer. We found the murder weapon and we also think that we might have found the victim's cottage."

"Tell us where?" Wayne asked eagerly.

"Way up the river, close to Windmill Lake. You can get to

it through the Happy Valley Adult Community park. It's part way down a steep path cut into the riverbank and is really concealed from view."

"Are you sure that the cottage belongs to the dead man?" Tom asked.

"No, to be honest, we haven't got a clue yet, but tomorrow we're going back to have a closer look."

"Best of luck, mate." Mike said and changed the subject. An hour and a half later Tom looked at his watch and realized that it was gone six.

"Right, I'm off, dinner calls. See you all next week and hopefully we'll see you too, John. Rose and I must have you around for dinner one night."

"That would be great," John said hesitantly, "see you again soon."

Rose had their dinner all ready and was just waiting for Tom to return. The fragrant smell of coq au vin wafted through the house. Tom finally came through the door apologizing for being late. Rose proceeded to serve their meal and they both tucked in heartily.

"Oh, by the way, love, DCI Hargreaves joined us at the Black Dog. They've found the murder weapon and think that they might have found the victim's cottage."

"Tell me, Tom. Where?" Rose said feeling suddenly quite excited.

"You know the adult community close to Windmill Lake on the Bayfield River Road, just up from the brewery? Well, down by the river there is apparently a small cottage hidden in the bush. They're going to take a look tomorrow."

"You know something, Tom, I used to know an elderly couple in the village who had a son; I think that his name was Hendrich. Well, Hendrich was autistic or certainly on the spectrum, but he was pretty well a science genius. I think that he had three or four degrees and was a doctor emeritus from Queen's University. I remember that, but what were his parent's names? Let me think, yes, they were Dutch. Umm... ah, that's it, Willie and Lora. They retired and left Bayfield almost fifteen years ago. I'm sure that their son had a cottage hidden away from the public eyes. It could be Hendrich, the victim I mean."

Tom looked thoughtful. "Well, I'm sure all will be revealed tomorrow, but changing the subject somewhat, love, Ian has invited us to join him at his cottage in Manitoulin. He's going there tomorrow and asked if we'd like to come for the weekend. What do you think, love?"

Rose had felt sorry for Ian who had been widowed now for two years. She had not met his wife Fiona who had been in declining health for many years. Ian had been invited over for dinner several times and Tom, of course, played golf with him on a regular basis. She knew how lonely he was and wished that they could do more to help him.

"Wow, that's short notice, but hey, that would be great, Tom. We'll have to book the Chi-Cheemaun ferry as this time of the year it starts to get pretty booked up."

"Good thinking, love. I'll do that right away. If we leave tomorrow, we could stay until Monday or Tuesday, couldn't we?"

"Well, no later than Tuesday, Tom, because Anne and the family will be arriving Thursday. Can we take the dogs?"

"I'll ask Ian, but if not, I'm sure that Kate would look after them."

"I'll ask her, but maybe you should contact Ian first."

"Okay, I'll ask Ian first and we'll take it from there, love." Tom said and disappeared off to his study to book the ferry.

A little while later Rose appeared popping her head around the study door. "Tom, where in Manitoulin is Ian's cottage?"

"Meldrum Bay, which is about a two-hour drive from where the ferry embarks."

"Gosh, that's just such a huge coincidence, Tom as I'm sure that Willie and Lora have a house on Meldrum Bay. If only I could remember their surnames."

"It will come to you, love. Meldrum Bay is only a small place. There can't be many Willies and Loras living there now, can there?"

"Yes, you're right. Anyway, if we find them, we can pop in and ask if Hendrich has a cottage by the river. Mind you, if it is his house that will mean that we would have to tell them that he might be dead and I can't do that, it would be awful."

"We could just ascertain if it's his house or not and leave it to the police to follow up, I suppose." Tom said dubiously, "Or we could just leave well enough alone and not look them up."

They were both quiet as they reflected on the possibilities. Rose let out a deep sigh and said, "Well, we'll face that when we come to it and not before."

Tom got up and began to clear the table. "Do you want a sherry, love?"

Rose had taken to drinking a sherry each night whilst watching television. It was her relaxation time and had become something of a ritual. She smiled at Tom and said, "Yes please, Tom. Let's go and sit down in the living room together and watch some television."

TEN

John was at the town hall a good half an hour before his team arrived. He had checked into The Little Inn the night before and, although his bed had been really comfortable, he had not slept at all well. Images of Rose as he had held her tight, the heat of her body melting into his, and the touch of her soft skin against his had kept him awake tossing and turning all night long. He was consumed with a desire so profound that his whole body literally ached for Rose, so much so that he actually welcomed the morning. Anything to take his mind off his unfulfilled love.

It was another beautiful day. As he walked up Main Street, he once again mused that Bayfield was a lovely village. If it hadn't been for Rachel, he would move here in an instant. But his daughter loved having her dad near her in London, even though much of that was the convenience of him being around to babysit. Also, he was the only family member she had left, and it was amazing to think that he had moved to Canada with the sole intention of being close to her. Maybe one day he would finally retire, and Bayfield would be his choice for retirement.

He reached the Town Hall and punched in the door code. Walking down to the basement he passed the small jail on the left opposite the kitchen. Rose had said that there had been a murder in the jail not so long ago, something about a stabbing with a kitchen knife. He would have to ask his team about that. For now, however, their priority was to establish the identity of the dead man and to solve his murder.

John opened his laptop and read his emails. There was a report from Doctor Green which pretty well said, but in a lot more words, that the dead man had died from massive brain injury. They would have to wait for the results of the blood work and the state of the organs. *Fair enough*, John thought, *now hurry up team*, "I want to get going." He had said that last bit out loud not realizing that Constable Ryan had just entered the room. She gave him a funny look.

"Talking to yourself, guv? You know what they say about that?"

John laughed, "It's a perennial past time of mine and hopefully I'm not going mad, yet."

Within five minutes the whole team was assembled and before they could get settled John said, "Okay, everyone, we're all going on an outing. I think that I've found where our victim lived. We're going to check it out. Let's take two cars as I don't want to alarm the residents of Happy Valley. Constable Ryan, you can ride with me."

Five minutes later the two cars were parked at the end of the road in the Happy Valley community. They could see the entrance to the pathway leading down to the river. John took the lead and the rest of his team followed. Almost at the end of the steep track, tucked behind some bushes, they could see the roof of the small shack. John pushed his way through the over-growth and found himself looking at quite a new front door. He tried the handle knob and found, to his astonishment, that it was not locked.

"Okay, everyone, remember this is a potential crime scene so do not disturb anything. The forensic and IDENT teams, not forgetting the SOC, will be along shortly and they will catalogue everything. What we're looking for is some kind of identification. We need to put a name to our victim."

"Look over here, guv." Holly said and pointed to what looked like a state of the art laboratory. A microscope sat on a stainless-steel table with several glass Petri dishes stacked to one side. Bundles of files were piled high on the floor and the whole wall was covered with books. John scanned some of the titles: *Micro-organisms in Water, Groundwater Contamination, PCBs in Water,* and *Pathogens and Contagions* being but a few.

In the corner of the room was a pair of fisherman's waders and a fishing net. There was also a small, free-standing aquarium which appeared to contain nothing but snails of all shapes and sizes. Everything was extremely neat and orderly. Other than a small bathroom and an equally small kitchen the only other room in the house was a bedroom.

Inside the bedroom a single bed, tidily made with an old-fashioned quilt on top, sat squarely next to a chest of draw-ers. An old-fashioned wind-up alarm clock sat on the chest of drawers. Other than an odd pair of socks and slippers placed under the bed and a thick plaid dressing gown hanging from a hook behind the door, there was very little else to see.

"Constable Ryan, go through his clothing and the chest of drawers and see if you can find anything to identify the man."

John felt his initial sense of excitement in discovering the cottage begin to ebb away.

The bathroom yielded nothing besides a sink with a razor blade, a shaving brush, a soap dish, toothbrush, and a squashed tube of toothpaste. There was no shower, just an old stained enamelled bathtub, with mouldy looking tiles around it.

"I'm going back to the main room." John said and returned to the pristine laboratory.

"Sir?" Constable Brown called. "Come and look at these research papers." He pointed to a bookcase stacked high with papers. "Most of them had obscure titles, but over half of them were written by Doctor Hendrich de Roo. Constable Brown pointed to one in particular, *Isotopes in Ground Water Source,* by Dr. Hendrich de Roo, Bayfield, Ontario. This could be our man, sir."

John nodded and looked more closely at the other research papers. The titles all pertained to water and microbes; some were from Cornell University, others from Harvard, Berkeley, London, or Oslo, and most were written over twenty years ago apart from four which were all dated between 2014 and present day. These were published through the University of Western, London, Ontario.

"Wow," John said, "this Dr. Hendrich was some academic. Constable Brown, have you found his computer yet?"

The laboratory was so tidy with everything neatly set out, test tubes in stands, petri dishes stacked, but there were no obvious signs of a computer anywhere. Constable Brown opened what looked like a cupboard but was in fact a walk-in storage room with tanks containing even more snails and, under what looked like an ultra-violet light, there wiggled hundreds of worms. Next to one of the glass tanks sat a small laptop computer.

"Here you are, sir," Constable Brown said," Should I leave it here for the forensic team?"

"Yes," John said, "We mustn't disturb anything else. They're on their way. I can hardly wait to open up the computer and see what our good doctor was up to, but right now I think that we've seen enough. We'll go back to the town hall and talk about what we've seen. A little bit of brain storming is required, and I want Constable Ryan, our computer genius, to find out as much as she can about Doctor Hendrich de Roo. Okay, team, time to leave."

ELEVEN

It was only after they had driven up to Tobermory and were aboard the Chi-Cheemaun ferry, that Rose suddenly remembered Willie and Lora's surname. "De Roo," she said out aloud and Tom looked at her strangely saying, "De Roo, what do you mean, love?"

"Oh, sorry Tom, it's just that I remembered Willie and Lora's name, you know the elderly couple I was telling you about whose son, Hendrich, had a house somewhere near the Bayfield River."

Tom still looked vague, but Rose persisted. "You know, the murder location and the small house nearby, well, that could be Willie and Lora's son Hendrich's house."

"A lot of could be's, love" Tom said sagely, "Let's go on deck and get some fresh air." Tom said getting up to go.

"Oh," Rose said, "I fancied getting something to eat from the restaurant. You go and get some air and I'll get us some lunch."

With that decided, Rose went down to the café and Tom went up to the viewing deck.

The crossing took almost two hours. Manitoulin Island was, according to the brochure Rose had been reading, the biggest freshwater island in the world, located on Lake Huron off the tip of the Bruce Peninsular which separated Georgian Bay from Lake Huron. Manitoulin stretched over 2766 square kilometres with over one hundred inland lakes dotted throughout the island.

They had been given the directions to Ian's cottage and it took another two hours of driving before they reached Meldrum Bay. Rose couldn't believe how remote the island felt. They had only passed two cars in the two hours of driving and both were in the small town of Providence Bay which was a lovely looking spot with a beautiful sandy beach. There were also hardly any shops, restaurants, or gas stations anywhere, although on reaching Meldrum Bay Rose was relieved to see a restaurant and a village shop which overlooked the colourful marina.

Ian's small cottage was tucked away off the road leading out of the village and looked out over the bay. Tom could see why Ian needed help as bushes and undergrowth had threatened to take over, so much so that the driveway was almost concealed.

Ian greeted them effusively and soon they were sitting on a wooden deck looking out over the bay drinking ice cold beers whilst listening to the water lap gently up against the jetty. *It is gloriously peaceful*, Rose thought, *a perfect place for a retreat.*

"I've made a reservation for us to have dinner at the Inn tonight." Ian said,

"And I've made a lasagne for tomorrow night's dinner, so we're all set." Rose said cheerfully. She looked around the bush and then added a little nervously,

"Tell me, Ian, are there many bears here?" It had certainly

looked very much like bear country on their drive over, there were just so many trees.

Ian laughed, "Don't tell me that you're frightened of bears, Rose."

"No, I'm not really frightened, it's just that they're very big and I'm not sure how I'd cope if one came charging at me."

"Well, in all the years we've been here I've only ever seen bears at a distance. Mind you, we have to be careful when barbequing. They get one whiff of meat cooking and boy, they'll soon come running."

"So, Ian, are you going to keep the cottage?" Rose asked as she sipped on her beer and looked out over the sparkling water. It truly was idyllic and so very relaxing listening to the sounds of the waves lapping against the jetty and the odd loon cry out.

Ian was quiet for a while and Rose thought that maybe he had not heard her. She was about to repeat her question when he answered. "No, I'm going to put it on the market at the end of the summer. This was Fiona's dream and without her this place feels empty." His eyes welled up and Rose wished that she hadn't brought up the subject.

Ian coughed and cleared his throat. "Still, we've had good times here and now they're all locked away in my memory. You know, Rose, there is a time and a place for everything in life and Fiona and I had our time here together. I'm also thinking of selling our house in Bayfield. I seem to rattle around in it now that's it's only just me."

"Oh, Ian, are you sure about selling your house? Where will you go?"

"I'm thinking of moving back to London. Our kids and grandchildren all live there and there are several condos for sale. I can still join Tom and the gang for the odd game of golf you know. Anyway, nothing's definite and first things first, this cottage needs tidying up and then it will go on the market. Right, it's time to go for dinner, are you two ready?"

They all got up and walked back up the steep bank to where the cottage nested like an eagle's nest. Rose quickly brushed her hair and then changed into a summer dress. Ian and Tom didn't bother to change. They both were wearing almost identical jeans and sweatshirts.

During the course of dinner at the Meldrum Bay Inn, Rose asked Ian if he knew the De Roo's. He hadn't heard of them, but called the waiter over, who also happened to be the owner of the Inn and asked him if he knew them.

"Why, of course I know Lora de Roo. Sadly, her husband, Willie, passed away two years ago. Can I ask why you ask?"

Rose smiled and said, "They're friends of mine from Bayfield. I knew that they had moved here about ten years ago and wondered if you had an address. I'd just love to see Lora again."

"Well, you're in luck as she lives just up the hill and around the corner. Shall I give her a call and let her know that you'll be visiting?"

"That would be so kind of you. Maybe you could ask if tomorrow morning at say nine-thirty would be a good time to visit?"

The landlord left the room and returned a few minutes later with a big smile on his face. "She said that anyone from Bayfield would be welcome and tomorrow morning would be just fine."

With that settled Tom, Ian and Rose continued to enjoy the rest of the evening eating a lovely meal of scallops sautéed in garlic butter served on a mound of pilaff and stir-fried vegetables. The wine flowed liberally and soon all maudlin thoughts were vanquished and replaced with a great sense of bonhomie.

Rose and Tom slept well that night with only the distant mournful sound of a loon and the occasional plop of a fish in the background.

TWELVE

The team was all assembled and there was a heightened sense of excitement in the room. DCI Hargreaves stood up to welcome everyone and then he proceeded to summarize what they had discovered in the small cottage by the Bayfield River.

"It appears that our John Doe," here John fished through his notebook before continuing, "has a name: Dr. Hendrich de Roo. It also appears that he was a scientist. From his biography and based on his recent research papers, we know he is, I mean *was*, a microbiologist and is particularly interested in water-borne pathogens.

Now that we know a little more about our victim, his identity being foremost, one has to ask the question, who would want to kill him? In other words what are the possible motives behind this murder? Any thoughts?"

The team was so quiet John thought that they had all gone to sleep. He was about to make a sarcastic remark about waking the dead when Sergeant Flowers finally spoke. "When you spoke of pathogens, sir, I immediately thought of germ warfare, you know, nasty viruses released into the air by some crazy terrorist or something like that. I know that it sounds far-fetched, but could our doctor have been developing something like that in his laboratory?"

John looked sceptical, but he nodded and said, "Good thinking, Sergeant, a bit James Bondish, but you could be onto something. Any more thoughts?"

Constable Ryan put her hand up. "I've been doing my own computer research on our doctor de Roo and boy, he's right up there with the best microbiologists in the world. According to one article I read, the man was pretty reclusive, rarely gave interviews, and shun public appearances only attending the most important conferences in the world. He hasn't made a public appearance in over ten years.

"According to Wikipedia, he is fifty-six years old, single, and a world specialist in microbiology. Oh, and there is something else, apparently twelve years ago he went on an expedition to the Amazon with eight other microbiologists. One of the group members almost died and was saved by Dr. de Roo who forced him to ingest controlled amounts of water purifying tablets. Our doctor later wrote up a paper about the use of potassium metabisulfite as a potential cure for pathogenic microbiotic diseases. There apparently was much controversy around this paper, and it appears that our good doctor lost a fair bit of credibility after publishing his paper. Other than that, guv, he seems to have gone off the radar these past few years."

"Thank you, Constable, we are still waiting for forensics to get back with the results of what they found on the computer. So far, we have not found a phone, and once again, we are waiting for forensics to get back to us on that."

John sighed. He just hated having to wait and wait for

results to come through; some investigations were really hampered by the waiting.

Constable Brown put up his hand.

"Yes Constable?"

"What about the log used to kill Doctor de Roo?"

"That is also with forensics. We have a lot of waiting to do, but in the meantime, let's continue our brainstorming. Any more ideas on possible motives for this murder?"

The room fell silent again.

Constable Elliot tentatively put up his hand.

"Well, sir, statistically most murders are family related. Did Hendrich have a family? Could it be something as simple as an argument gone wrong?"

"As far as we can see, Constable, our victim was an only child. His parents," here John referred to his notes again, "yes, his parents, Willie and Lora de Roo, lived in Bayfield from 1985 until 2009. They moved to Manitoulin Island after Willie retired where, I believe, they are still living."

Constable Ryan interrupted him by saying, "Well, actually no, guv, his dad, Willie, died a couple of years ago, but you're right, his mom is still living. I have an address for you in Meldrum Bay."

"Thank you, Holly. One of us will have to go to break the news to his mother; Sergeant Flowers, maybe you could do this. Look into flying up there as I believe Gore Bay has a small airport. See if you can fly from Kincardine on a chartered flight, otherwise you'll be going over on the Chee-Cheemaun and spending a full day getting there and back.

"Right, where were we? Ah, yes, the family angle, not to be dismissed lightly. Constable Elliot, I give you the task of looking into the extended family, you know, cousins, aunts, uncles, and grandparents; you get the picture, just don't leave any stone unturned.

"Constable Brown. Ask around the village and see if you can find anyone who knew the de Roo's, I'd like to get a clearer profile. Okay, we'll meet again tomorrow, eight o'clock."

The team ambled up the stairs from the basement, opened the door to the outside and were suddenly blinded by the bright sunshine. It was, after all, a beautiful summer's day. *Time for a quick pint*, John thought as he walked across Clan Gregor Square towards the Albion.

THIRTEEN

Rose woke up just as the sun was rising. Tom was still asleep, snoring gently, as she crept out of bed and made her way to the kitchen where she grabbed the kettle, filled it with water, and then went outside onto the deck overlooking the lake.

She loved this time of the day with the stillness and peacefulness which appeared to soak into her very being. A couple of loons appeared on the still water of the bay and then disappeared again. The water lapped gently against the dock and Rose was at utter peace with the world, so that when Ian came up behind her, she fairly jumped out of her skin.

"Oh, good morning, Ian, you made me jump. I do hope that I didn't disturb you. Would you like a cup of tea; I'm just about to make a pot."

"Thank you, Rose. Actually, I'm a coffee man, but what I came out for was to check if the porcupine has been back? He's taken to chewing the wood on the edge of the deck."

Ian pointed to the side of the wooden deck and sure enough Rose could see great gauges chewed out of the wood.

"Wow, I never thought that porcupines could be so destructive."

"So, Rose, how do you like Manitoulin Island?"

"Well, there are an awful lot of trees and forests here, but it is very restful."

Ian smiled and then said, "If you were in Japan, you would be taking in the forest atmosphere or, as they say, forest bathing. I think the Japanese have an expression for it, shinrin-yoku. It was developed in the 1980's and has become a cornerstone of preventive medicine.

"Apparently, research in both Japan and South Korea had established proven scientific health benefits of spending time in a forest. It's supposed to boost the immune system, reduce blood pressure and stress, improve moods, and increase energy levels. So, there you are, Rose, you should spend the day in the forest."

"Not on your life, the bears would find me, I'm sure." Rose laughed and Ian joined in.

Tom must have heard them talking and laughing because a few minutes later he emerged from the cottage and joined them on the deck looking decidedly blurry eyed and tussled. Rose went inside to make the tea and coffee leaving the men to talk.

An hour and a half later, after a huge breakfast of bacon, sausage, eggs, and fries, Rose left the men clearing brush and walked back to Meldrum Bay.

When she reached the Inn, she walked up the steep hill at the corner and found Lora de Roo's house. It was so charming that Rose just stood in front admiring the delightful little house which was as pretty as a post card. It was like something out of *Anne of Green Gables* with bright yellow clapboard and white gingerbread trim surrounded by a wrap-around porch with neat flower boxes attached to the railings. A white picket fence completed the picture- perfect façade.

Rose walked up to the front door and was about to knock when the door was opened abruptly by Lora. Had she not known that she was at the de Roo's address Rose would never have recognized Lora. In front of her stood a small, diminutive old lady with a mass of shocking white hair. However, the minute that she smiled the old Lora Rose had remembered, seemed to shine through.

"Ah, Rose Blair, how good to see you again after all these years. You're looking good, my dear, come on in."

She followed Lora into a cosy living room. There were framed pictures of Willie and Lora together and one large picture of a young, handsome man wearing a graduation gown bearing a Queens University logo. *That must be Hendrich,* thought Rose as she sat down on the sofa.

"So how is everyone in Bayfield?" Lora asked, "Is the croquet club still going strong?"

They talked for a while about life in the village before Rose asked Lora if she had heard from Hendrich recently.

Lora sighed and then said, "I can sometimes go months without hearing from him. I know that when he's involved in a new project, he becomes so focused on his work that nothing else exists for him. When Willie died two years ago, I had to contact a friend of mine from Bayfield to go and find Hendrich and let him know that his father had died. He just wasn't answering his phone."

"Does he still live somewhere near the Bayfield River?" Rose asked tentatively.

"Yes, and that's another thing that Willie and I always fretted about. His house is so close to the riverbank, literally feet away from the water and it's so isolated. But Hendrich has never listened to us. He says that he loves the fact that he is away from people and, as most of his research pertains to water, it made perfect sense for him to live so close to the river. You know something, Rose, our son is just plain and simply stubborn and anti-social too." Lora laughed and got up to put the kettle on for tea.

When she returned with a tray and teapot covered in a bright red knitted tea cosy, two china cups and saucers, and a plate of homemade cookies, Rose had to smile. Lora was the epitome of a good hostess even though she had to be in her late seventies, maybe already eighty.

"I was sorry to hear about Willie's death, Lora; it must be very lonely for you living out here all by yourself."

"Actually, you would be surprised what a busy community Meldrum Bay is, particularly in the summer. I also run an Airbnb business and have two bedrooms that are constantly booked throughout the summer, so I keep myself busy. Rose, could I ask a favour of you? Would you go and visit Hendrich and let him know that his old mom would appreciate a phone call from him."

"Of course, I can do that Lora. But how do I get to his house?"

"Oh, if you drive down Bayfield River Road past Carriage Lane and the Old Homestead and continue down past Orchard Line you will come to the Happy Valley Adult Community. Just drive in through the trailer park right to the end of the road and then you have to leave your car and walk down a rather steep path towards the river. His house is on the right hidden behind some bushes."

"Of course, I can do that for you, Lora. Do you have his telephone number and could I have your telephone number?"

Lora got a notepad and wrote down both her and

Hendrich's telephone numbers as well as her address. She looked up and said, "I'll give you my email address as well." This gave Rose pause for thought. Fancy an eighty-year-old being so into technology. Next, she would be hearing that she used social media too, *but then again, if she did Airbnb, she would have to use the internet for communication, wouldn't she,* Rose mused, suitably impressed.

"Does Hendrich not email you then if he doesn't phone?"

Lora let out another deep sigh. "No, Rose, he just doesn't communicate well at all, I've given up leaving emails and telephone messages, when he's ready I know that he will be in touch."

Rose had a sinking feeling, it was beginning to feel more and more likely that the man washed up on the Flats could very well be Hendrich. So, with a very heavy heart Rose took her leave from Lora de Roo knowing that in all likelihood the poor woman would very soon be mourning the loss of another loved one.

FOURTEEN

DCI Hargreaves had spent the afternoon reading through a stack of research papers all penned by Doctor Hendrich de Roo. The general thrust of his work centred around pathogens, particularly parasitology and waterborne pathogens like cholera.

Some of the papers talked about predicting patterns and in some a Dr. Chen from Sichuan University talked about the control and spreading of pathogens which then became very complicated and began to lose John with all the academic references.

He found himself nodding off and was abruptly awakened by his telephone. It was Kate, Rose's sister, whom he had been talking to at the Albion over lunch.

"Is that you, John?" she shouted down the phone. John held the phone away from his ear and said, "Yes, it is I."

"Oh, John, I wondered if you might like to come to my place for dinner tonight?"

John was a bit taken aback as it was Rose whom he craved and not her sister, but he couldn't come up with an excuse quick enough and so he found himself saying, "That would be great. What time?"

"About six-thirty would be just fine."

John put his phone down and said out loud. "Oh, shit, what have I done?"

FIFTEEN

Two days previously and seventy kilometres away in the village of Ilderton, just outside London, Doctor Deb Cane had put her phone down with much the same sentiment as John. She had tried to reach Hendrich de Roo for about the tenth time that day and every time the phone had gone to voicemail until there was no further room on the messaging system to take her calls.

Wherever he was, he certainly was not picking up his phone. But then there was nothing new about that as he was possibly the world's worst communicator. How a man of such intellect could be so oblivious to other people thoroughly intrigued Deb. She knew that in all likelihood he was probably engrossed in one of his laboratory experiments and was off in his own world of academia, but she really did need to get a hold of him.

Deb had known Hendrich for ten years. He had been the advisor for her doctorate and her mentor ever since. They had collaborated in several research papers together and were currently working on another. It was for this reason that she desperately needed to get in touch with him as her science research grant was running out and the paper had to be submitted by the following week. She had tried emailing, texting, and phoning and none had elicited any response. If all else failed, she would have to drive to his place in Bayfield as she really wanted Hendrich to read through the paper before submission.

Deb scrolled through her emails one more time and scanned the multitude of questions and queries that she received on a daily basis from her students. Eventually she found an email from Hendrich dated two weeks previous and she realized that it had been that long since she had received any communication from him.

Whilst Hendrich was a man of few words he had in the past been diligent about any academic work and questions pertaining to such. Unless, Deb thought, he was on to something and then he could lose himself for days on end. She decided that the only thing for it was to take a drive to Bayfield and meet up with the professor in person.

Now, two days later, Deb was aware that she really needed to pick up her flash drive which she had foolishly left behind at her last visit with the professor. It was vital that she got a hold of the comments that he had promised to make on her draft of their paper.

It was a stunningly beautiful day, sunny with a clear blue sky, and the drive from Ilderton to Bayfield was a breeze, taking just over forty minutes.

Crossing the temporary bridge located to the west of the new bridge under construction, Deb looked down at the new abutments and found it hard to visualize what the new bridge would look like on completion.

Turning right on Old River Road she drove up the hill

through a canopy of trees and stopped at the stop sign. Sawmill Creek Trail was to her right and straight ahead was Carriage Lane where, turning left along the brick paved road, she continued on past the large homes. Eventually she came out on to Bayfield River Road and turning right opposite the Old Homestead, she drove on past the River Road Brewery towards Windmill Lake.

Before she reached the lake, a sign reading Happy Valley Adult Community loomed large on her right. Deb drove into the trailer park, leaving her car parked at the top of the riverbank she walked down towards Hendrich's cottage. It was soon apparent that something was definitely amiss as yellow police tape fluttered in the wind and encircled Hendrich's house. An area down by the dock with flattened grass was also taped off. *What on earth is going on here?* Deb thought as she stood by the riverbank wondering what she should do.

As if in answer to her question a tall and rather handsome black man suddenly appeared from Hendrich's house followed by three other men and one woman. The tall man approached Deb. "Can I help you?"

He spoke with a very strong southern English accent, probably a Londoner. Deb looked around her and gestured with her hands at the yellow police tape. "What's happening here? Why is police tape everywhere? I came to visit Hendrich. Where is he?"

Her voice had risen a few notches and DCI Hargreaves could see the panic rising in her eyes. He had seen that look so many times before on loved one's faces when they were about to be told of the death of their loved one. He put out his hand and said gently, "Could you come with me, ma'am, back to the village, we have set up an incident room in the Bayfield Town Hall. I'm afraid I have some bad news for you, and I need to ask you some questions about Doctor de Roo. I'm DCI John Hargreaves and these are Sergeant Flowers, Constables Brown, Elliot, and Constable Ryan. We were just about to head back there ourselves."

Deb felt panicky, confused, and somewhat speechless as she followed the police back up to the top of the bank and then noticed the two other cars parked just down the road from where she had left her car. They drove off and she followed behind.

Once at the town hall, they all traipsed down to the basement and John pulled out a chair for Deb.

"Right, umm, Miss, I'm sorry, I didn't get your name?"

"It's Cave, Doctor Deborah Cave."

"Right, thank you, Doctor Cave; I have a few questions to ask you, but before I do would you please look at these photographs and confirm whether they are indeed of Dr. Hendrich de Roo."

Deb nodded her head and John took two prints out of a brown envelope. They were the most sanitized pictures of the victim that he could find. After his face had been cleaned up, Hendrich looked quite peaceful in death.

Deb looked at the two photographs and then let out a gasp. "You mean to tell me that Hendrich is dead? Oh my God, how on earth did it happen?"

John gave a brief summary of how they had found him, omitting the grizzly details.

Deb interrupted him. "So, he drowned? I knew something like this would happen one day as he spent his life taking samples from that bloody river. His research meant everything to him and now it's finally taken his life." Tears started to roll down her cheeks. "I'm sorry, I'm not usually so emotional, but Hendrich was such a good, kind man and a genius too."

"Don't apologize," John said kindly, "you're in shock and quite understandably upset. I'm sorry that I had to show you the photographs, but you see, we also needed confirmation that this is indeed Hendrich de Roo. Now Deborah, if you don't mind me calling you by your first name, would you mind if I asked you a few questions about him?"

Deb sniffed and said, "Sure. It's Deb actually but go ahead."

"Thanks Deb, so how long had you known him?"

Deb thought for a minute and then answered, "Well, he was an advisor for my doctorate thesis at Western University. That was ten years ago, but since then we've worked together on several research papers. He was helping me with my current paper which is why I came down to meet him."

John looked up from his notebook where he had been writing, "You had a meeting set up with him? When were you going to meet?"

Deb shook her head and said, "No, I didn't actually have a meeting set up, but I've been trying to get a hold of him for several weeks. He never returned any of my calls or emails and so I decided that maybe he was too engrossed in his lab work and hadn't checked his emails. He's like that, a real absent-minded professor."

"What was Hendrich working on? I gather from all the research papers in his laboratory that it was something to do with water and pathogens. Could you elaborate on this, please?"

"Oh, gee, well how long have you got? I could talk for hours, but basically Hendrich was concerned about the increase in pathogens in the Bayfield River. You've obviously heard of Lyme disease, and you probably associate that with ticks and rightly so, but what you probably don't know is that the tick is just the host for the pathogen, which is the bacterium Borrelia burgdorferi transmitted to humans and other animals through the bite of an infected blacklegged tick.

"There are snails that live in the riverbank reeds and grasses and those same snails, like the ticks, are hosts to a number of microscopic pathogens which are so tiny that they can be absorbed into the pores of human tissue. If not diagnosed and treated immediately they then run amok with the organs of the body. Hendrick has spent years and years researching these pathogens and he may have possibly even found a cure for some of the nastier diseases like Lyme and Bilharzia."

John interrupted her briefly, "Are these nasty pathogens just found in the Bayfield River?"

"Oh no, no, no. Hendrich first came across some of them when he was on a science research expedition up the Amazon River and then later, when he was in Africa on the Zambezi River. Of course, the tropics are rife for all sorts of pathogens, both water and air born. Malaria which is carried by the mosquito is the most common deadly pathogen and then there's the Tsetsi fly, which causes sleeping sickness.

"Basically, pathogens fall into five different groups: viruses, fungi, bacteria, and the parasite protozoa and helminths. E-coli is caused from faecal contaminated water, as is cholera, oh, and don't forget the black plague was spread by pathogens living on fleas. The world, detective is a scary place, very scary and it's going to get a lot worse with climate change."

John and his team looked suitably shocked and were all very quiet as they digested the information. *How could any of this be related to Hendrich's death?* thought John as he prepared to tell Doctor Cave that her associate Doctor de Roo had actually been murdered.

"So, Doctor Cave, do you know of anyone who might have had it in for Hendrich?"

Deb looked shocked and then thoughtful. "There is a pharmaceutical company just outside of Brampton which Hendrich mentioned to me on more than one occasion. He was getting the run around from one of the CEOs. That is the only thing that comes to mind as you must have realized by now that Hendrich led a pretty reclusive life out here. If you ask me, I think that he was probably autistic, or certainly on the spectrum."

"Thank you, Doctor Cave. You've been most helpful, if we need to speak to you again could you leave your contact details here with Constable Holly Ryan?"

"Yes, sure," Deb said and proceeded to hand a card over to Holly.

"Well, if that's all, I'll be on my way. Oh, I've just thought of something important. Hendrich has a mother who lives somewhere on Manitoulin Island. She'll need to be notified."

"We're on to it." Sergeant Flowers said and shook hands with Deb. John followed her up the stairs and showed her out. "You really have been a great help to us. Thank you."

Deb smiled and headed over to her car feeling still quite numbed by the morning's events.

SIXTEEN

K ate had spent a glorious afternoon preparing for her dinner date with John. Like her sister, Rose, she had always found cooking to be a great balm to the soul. Other than having Rose and Tom around for supper occasionally, she had little opportunity to show off her culinary skills and so she had gone rather overboard. A Moroccan lamb Tagine simmered gently in the oven letting out sweet smelling aromas of rosemary and thyme, while eggplant parmigiana was prepared and ready to be sautéed. Flat breads and a selection of dips nestled on the coffee table along with black and green olives.

Kate had made three different desserts: a chocolate mousse, a lemon tart, and finally a stack of profiteroles just oozing with cream and chocolate. She looked at her watch and realized that she had just thirty minutes before John would be arriving, time enough to get smartened up or, and here she deliberated, she could take the dogs for a walk. Rose and Tom had dropped off Ben and Puff before heading off to Manitoulin

Island, and together with Lucy, her little fox hound terrier, her house had been turned into a veritable doghouse.

Typically, the dogs won her over, and so grabbing their leashes Kate called all three. "Just a quick walk around the block, darlings," Kate said as she was pulled to the front door by all three dogs keen to be on their way.

It was a beautiful summers evening, the air was clean and crisp, the dreadful humidity that had embraced the whole of Ontario for two weeks now had suddenly lifted. The leaves on the trees were a lush green and pansies were flowering everywhere, as were the dandelions.

Kate walked past Rose and Tom's house on Bayfield Terrace to Catherine Street where she turned left onto Colina Street even though the dogs had tried to steer her in the direction of the lake.

"We don't have time, darlings for the beach today, maybe tomorrow." she said and once again looked at her watch. Arriving back at her house with just five minutes to spare, Kate rushed into her bedroom, brushed her hair, and quickly put on some lipstick. Her jeans and t-shirt would just have to do. Bang on time, there was a knock on the door and all three dogs rushed to the door, barking simultaneously. Kate opened the door and John entered to a cacophony of barking dogs. Once John started to stroke Puff and Ben they stopped, and peace was regained.

"Good boys, you remember me, don't you?"

Lucy nudged his hand as if to say, what about me?

"How come you have Rose and Tom's dogs, Kate?"

"Oh, they've gone away for a few days to Manitoulin Island. Actually, they should be back tomorrow. Come into the sitting room and I'll get you a drink."

John looked around the cosy room. It was decorated with

brightly coloured rugs and modern art hanging on all the walls. The sofa was smothered with exotic cushions, and ceramic bowls containing olives and various dips sat on a circular low-level coffee table.

"This is charming, Kate. Umm... do you have a beer?"

With drinks sorted out, Kate curled up on the sofa and John sat on a modern brown leather Ikea chair, while Puff, Ben, and Lucy joined Kate on the sofa. From the side of the chair a tiny, fluffy kitten appeared, and Lucy jumped off the sofa and nudged the kitten gently with her nose. John watched astonished as Lucy grabbed the little fluff ball in her mouth and jumped back on the sofa laying the kitten down by her side. Kate laughed at the expression on John's face,

"My, just look at you, don't look so shocked. Hey, don't worry, Lucy just thinks that she's Miffy's mother, they're actually inseparable."

"That's amazing, "John said.

Appraising Kate from across the room, he had to admit that she looked pretty good and appeared far less vulnerable and fragile than she had the previous year after her separation from her husband, Bob. Then she had narrowly escaped being drowned by the Dutchman who had finally been arrested for the murder at Windmill Lake.

Physically the two sisters were not at all alike. Rose was smaller and rounder whereas Kate was taller and more angular. They both however had the same almond shaped green eyes and wide sensuous mouths.

"Anyway, how've you been, John? I can't believe that it's been almost a year since I last saw you and now, you're back here investigating another murder. How is that going?"

"Well, at least we can finally put a name to our victim.

We're still waiting for forensics, but we are definitely looking at murder."

"So, who is your victim?"

"His name is Hendrich de Roo, and he lived in a small cottage by the side of the Bayfield River."

"Gosh, John, you don't mean Doctor Hendrich de Roo, do you?"

"Yes, but why, did you know him?"

"Well, no, I didn't, but my daughter, Ally knew him. He was one of her lecturers at university. Actually, she really liked him, and I just know that she'll be very upset to hear of his demise."

"So, what did your daughter study at university?" John asked.

"Ally originally wanted to study medicine and then she got really interested in microbiology. Dr. de Roo was her hero. She used to tell me some of the stories that he regaled from when he was in the Amazon and then in Africa. He was a world-renowned scientist and I'm sure that he'll be missed greatly in the academic world."

"Is your daughter still at university?"

Kate shook her head, "No, she graduated a couple of years ago and now lives in Australia. She got a position as a researcher at the University of Melbourne."

"That's a long way to go and visit. Have you been out there yet?"

"I was there during Christmas, and it was fabulous. She's met a hunky Aussie and seems very happy and that's all that matters. Now, let's go and eat, I'm starving."

Over dinner John managed to get Kate to open up about her life in Kelowna and how she and her ex had run a farm full of pets including llamas, a donkey, goats, and pot-bellied pigs.

She talked about her husband going off with her best friend Natalie and how it had come as such a shock when she had found out, particularly as she had had no inkling that they had been carrying on behind her back for a whole year before she had found out.

John found himself opening up to Kate about the loss of his wife, Fiona, and how their only child, Rachel had brought forward her wedding so that Fiona could see her daughter walk down the aisle. Sadly, she had died before seeing any grandchildren and before Rachel and her husband had moved to Canada.

By the end of the meal both Kate and John were feeling very comfortable with each other. The dinner had been a wonderful interlude to an otherwise frustrating week.

SEVENTEEN

Rose and Tom boarded the Chi-Cheemaun ferry and settled down for the two-hour crossing. Although their two days away had been very relaxing, they were both looking forward to going home.

Rose was anxious to pass on what she had learnt about Hendrich de Roo to John Hargreaves, even though it would mean meeting with him again which made Rose feel more than a little apprehensive. As to Tom, he had enjoyed helping Ian clean up the property and had also revelled in the peacefulness of Manitoulin Island, although both of them had missed their beloved dogs and were looking forward to seeing them again.

Instead of taking the early morning ferry the next day, which would have required them leaving Meldrum Bay by six thirty in the morning, Rose and Tom had decided to opt for the afternoon crossing which would get them back to Tobermory by six and home to Bayfield by about nine that evening.

Sitting in the lounge of the Chi-Cheemaun Ferry Rose browsed through a tourist brochure on the Bruce Peninsula.

She nudged Tom who had been drifting off to sleep and said, "Listen to this Tom. There was a time, according to First Nations folk lore, when lake levels were so low that people could walk from the tip of the Bruce Peninsular across to Manitoulin Island. Science now confirms this because beneath the waters of Georgian Bay lie the remains of prehistoric forests. Isn't that interesting Tom?"

Tom nodded and shook his head. He hadn't really been listening to Rose, but now looking at the brochure in her hand he added, "Apparently after the last ice age the water in the Great Lakes fluctuated wildly. About seven thousand years ago, post glacial Lake Nipissing filled the Huron-Superior-Michigan basin with a water level much higher than today's lake levels. This elevated water level helped sculpt many of the features like Flowerpot Island, the sea caves, ledges, and much more. Just shows, Rose, that our lakes keep changing."

By the time Tom pulled up to their driveway they were both really tired, but Rose insisted that they pick up the dogs from Kate's house and so they drove straight over to Louisa Street.

"That looks like DCI Hargreaves car." Tom said as he pulled into the drive, "I wonder what he's doing here?"

They knocked on the front door and were greeted by barking dogs. A rather flushed and slightly tipsy looking Kate appeared, "Oh, Rose, Tom, you're back, I wasn't expecting you tonight. Is everything okay?"

Puff and Ben came charging into the hall crazy with delight; Lucy followed, took one look, and then went back to the sofa where John and Miffy were sitting. Rose and Tom entered the living room. As soon as Rose set eyes on John, she began to feel both awkward and uncomfortable.

"Oh, John, I hope that we weren't interrupting anything?"

John stood up and gestured to the dining table where the remains of their meal still sat where they had left it.

"Your sister is an excellent cook; we've just had a superb dinner. What about you and Tom? Did you have a good time in Manitoulin?"

Rose nodded her head and forced herself to smile. "Yes, it was lovely, but John, I have some information for you about your murder victim, Hendrich de Roo. I met with his mom, Lora, and I had a long chat about him. Sadly, she doesn't yet know that he's dead."

John replied, "I know. I've despatched Sergeant Flowers to Manitoulin to break the news to her."

"That's good, John. Did you find Hendrich's house? His mom said that he liked the seclusion, but she was always worried that he might drown, or his home get flooded because it was so close to the water. So, tell me do you have a motive yet for his murder? Have forensics given you a time of death?"

John smiled. Rose certainly knew how the system worked. He answered her questions patiently,

"Hopefully, we'll hear back from them tomorrow. I'm also waiting for a summary of the contents from Hendrich's computer. Everything always takes time and, in the end, it just becomes a waiting game."

Tom stood up and gently took Rose's arm. "We need to be getting home, love. I'll put the dogs in the car. Nice seeing you again, John, and don't be a stranger, come around for drinks one night."

"Thanks, Kate, for looking after the dogs. Look, I'll call you tomorrow." Rose hastily said and then she turned to John and said, "Umm... bye, John."

Rose departed feeling all flustered, she had much to think about and wasn't sure of her confused emotions.

EIGHTEEN

The team were all assembled and waiting when John finally arrived. He had woken up with a massive hangover and a throbbing headache having consumed more than two bottles of wine between them the night before at Kate's. He checked his laptop before setting off that morning and was pleased to see two reports from forensics: one from Doctor Green with an attachment from the Toronto Forensic Department, and the other report containing the down loaded correspondence from Hendrich de Roo's computer.

"Good morning everyone. You'll be pleased to hear that I finally have results from forensics. First, cause of death, no surprises here, acute intracerebral haemorrhage, with time of death estimated to be between five-thirty and seven o'clock. The body was found at seven thirty-five the following morning. Doctor Green estimated that the body had been in the water for at least twelve hours. It looks like our victim was attacked with a log and then his body was thrown into the river.

"Now here is the interesting bit. When Doctor Green conducted his post-mortem, he was shocked by the state of the victim's organs. As a consequence, he sent the body to the Toronto Forensics Unit to be analysed more thoroughly. The results are unusual to say the least, the liver, kidneys, and lungs show signs of extreme cirrhosis. It appears that the doctor was suffering both bilharzia and Lyme disease, as well as evidence of severe toxicity from exposure to PCBs. There were traces of sodium chlorite in his blood and a very low white platelet count. According to Doctor Green, Hendrich de Roo should have been dead long before he was killed.

"Okay, so now onto the computer print outs, there are a huge number of emails mostly from a pharmaceutical company called Santé. I looked them up and they're located near Brampton and are a well-established company with a sound reputation.

"Anyway, it appears that Hendrich was convinced that he had found the cure-all for a number of nasty diseases including Lyme, bilharzia, and a form of blood cancer. It is obvious from the tone of the emails that Santé did not share the same belief and refused to even read his research paper pertaining to the study.

"The last dozen emails written by the CEO himself, a Mr. Barry Brown, have a distinctly threatening tone. We need to interview this man because right now he appears to be our one and only potential suspect.

"Constable Ryan, I'm tasking you with the job of going through all these emails to see if anything else needs to be flagged. Constables Brown and Elliot, I would like you to drive to Brampton and interview this Barry Brown.

"I'm going to continue to read all these research papers and see if they can shed some light on what's going on.

Sergeant Flowers should be back tomorrow from Manitoulin. We won't meet tomorrow so let's see if we can get this all wrapped quickly. I feel that we are definitely onto something with this pharmaceutical company. Go to it everyone and bring me back some results."

Constables Brown and Elliot packed up and went upstairs and out into bright sunshine. They were beginning to feel a bit like Hobbits being stuck in the darkness of the basement room.

DCI Hargreaves picked up one of the research papers written by Doctor Hendrich de Roo, pulled on his glasses and started to read.

NINETEEN

The previous evening Rose had prepared a light supper for Tom and then, after settling the dogs down and alone with her thoughts in bed, Rose was able to analyse her feelings and jumbled emotions. Seeing her lovely sister Kate and John together had disturbed her equilibrium and Rose didn't like what she was feeling, and that was plain and simple jealousy.

It was absolutely ridiculous, Rose thought, to feel that way and so totally unjustified as John and Kate were both free to see each other. She after all was a happily married woman and definitely not in the market for an adulterous relationship.

Yet a little voice inside of her niggled away at her conscience. She wanted to confront Kate, to tell her to back off. John was hers. But of course, she would not, and indeed could never do that and she really should be thrilled that Kate and John were getting together as a couple. She should be giving them both her blessings, not thinking mean, jealous thoughts.

What is wrong with me? Rose thought. She had made her

choice when it had become clear that they had a strong physical attraction for each other.

Indeed, she was the one who had declared that she could not, and indeed, would not, have an affair and risk hurting Tom.

Silly me, Rose thought, *I'm behaving like a lovesick teenager.* "Get a grip," she said out aloud.

"Did you say something, love?" Tom said groggily. He had just fallen asleep and was not quite fully awake.

"Umm...no, darling, go back to sleep."

Rose finally fell asleep and woke that morning feeling as if she had put all her cares behind her. She got up and made breakfast whilst checking her planner to see what she had planned for the day ahead. She was going around to Susan's condo and then they both planned to drive out to have a look at Hendrich de Roo's house. *I'll make some muffins to take around to Susan's*, Rose thought as she pulled out her mixing bowl. *Now what type should I make?*

In the end she decided that chocolate muffins loaded with chocolate chips would go down well. She proceeded to mix the oil, cocoa, sugar, flour, and eggs together. Tom came into the kitchen and asked if there was anything that he could do before heading out to play golf?

"No thank you, darling." Rose said and gave him a quick kiss. "Will you be back for lunch?"

Tom shook his head and said, "No, I'll probably end up having a beer or two at the clubhouse. I'll be home by about three" He bent down and gave Rose a quick kiss. Just then the phone rang. Tom waved his hand and left the house leaving Rose to take the call. It was a very distressed Lora de Roo.

"Rose, it's Lora." There was a pause and then a loud sniff

before she continued to talk. "Did you know that Hendrich was already dead when you visited me?"

Rose went still. "No, I didn't know for sure, Lora, but I had my strong suspicions when I heard that the victim lived upstream of the Bayfield River bridge. I had remembered that your son had a place by the river, but I honestly didn't know for sure. I am so very sorry, Lora, so very sorry."

"They said that he was murdered. Oh Rose, who would do such a thing to my son?" There was another sob on the other end of the line.

"Lora, the police will find out who did this, I just know they will. But in the meantime, is there anything that I can do?"

"You can find out who did it, that's what you can do. I will not sleep until I know why my son was murdered. He was such a kind and generous man and a genius in his field. He didn't deserve to die."

There followed a bout of soul racking tears that broke Rose's heart.

"I'm sorry Rose, it's just that I feel so useless here. Do you know, they won't even release his body so I can't even bury him, my son, my own flesh and blood."

"Lora, if you want to come here and stay with us you know that you will be most welcome."

"Thank you, Rose, but I'll wait and see. I would really like to lay Hendrich to rest next to his father here in the Meldrum Bay Anglican Church cemetery."

"And so you shall, Lora, so you shall, all in good time."

They talked a little longer and then Lora said that she had to go, and Rose put the phone down feeling so heavy of heart that she almost burst into tears. The smell of muffins, however, almost burning, brought her back to her senses. She managed to save the muffins just before they started to blacken.

By the time that she got to Susan's condo her spirits had risen and she looked forward to a strong cup of coffee and a chat with her friend.

Arriving at her front door Rose was greeted by Susan who had the little white kitten cradled in her arms sound asleep like a baby.

"Come in, Rose," Susan whispered, "I'll just put Fluffy in her basket and then make us some coffee."

Rose looked around her friend's condo. There was a large black and white photograph of a herd of African elephants which hung over the stone fireplace, a brown leather L-shaped sofa graced the living room with a colourful Persian rug in the middle, and a wicker basket filled with cat toys sat by the fireplace.

"So, how are things going with Miffy, oops, I mean Fluffy?"

"Oh, I absolutely adore her, Rose. I can't believe that I've never had a kitten before; she's just constant entertainment. I swear that I get nothing done all day as I spend most of my time playing with her."

Rose reached into her bag and brought out a zip-lock bag. "Here, Susan, I baked these muffins for us to have with our coffee. After that I wonder if we could both take a drive up the road to see where Hendrich lived?"

Susan looked blank. Rose rushed in to explain.

"Oh, I'm sorry Susan, I always forget that you're no longer in the know with police work."

She spent the next few minutes getting Susan up to speed on what she knew about the Hendrich de Roo murder, concluding with, "So you see, Lora, Hendrich's mom, asked me to look into it and so now I feel morally obliged to do what I can."

Susan let out a loud guffaw. "Oh Rose, here you go again. You haven't changed a bit, have you? Hey, but you can count me in as I need something to do other than play with Fluffy, otherwise I'll just go plain stir crazy."

The two women drove down River Road, past the Old Homestead and the River Road Brewery, until they reached The Happy Valley Adult Community.

"Gosh, I didn't know that this place even existed." Susan said as they pulled in and drove past neat and very well cared for trailers nestled under tall pine trees.

"It's really cool," Susan added as Rose parked her Volvo, the two women got out of the car and walked towards the river embankment.

"It's pretty steep here, but there is actually a defined foot path of sorts. I wonder if Hendrich possessed a car."

Approaching the bottom of the steep embankment they could see the top of a small house.

"That must be where he lived." Susan said pointing to the roof. "It's pretty overgrown and well concealed. He must have really wanted to preserve his privacy."

Yellow police tape fluttered in the light breeze. The whole of the landing by the river had been cordoned off with tape.

"You said that he had been hit on the back of his head and then pushed into the river?" Susan said while she surveyed the site.

"Well, I don't know any details only what Tom told me. He had been having a beer with John, umm...I mean DCI Hargreaves, and that's when he got most of the information I know."

"You mean to say, Rose that you haven't had John around

for dinner yet and questioned him yourself? That's not like you."

Rose blushed, "Well, last year he came around several times and we got to know him quite well."

"Rose, you're blushing. Don't tell me you fancy the man. Gosh, Rose, you of all people, I don't believe it."

"I suppose that I do find him attractive, but don't worry I'm not about to jump into bed with the man. I'm happily married to Tom and anyhow I think that my sister Kate has set her sights on him."

"But Rose, how will we get information if you don't have an in with the handsome DCI? I tell you what, I'm going to invite him around for dinner myself, I will ply him with drinks and then interrogate the poor man until I get the whole case history out of him."

Rose laughed, "Way to go, girl."

They made a high five and then started to walk back up the bank. When they reached the top Rose noticed an elderly woman mowing the grass in front of her trailer. She walked over and feigning innocence, asked, "Hello, we were just wondering what all the yellow tape down by the river is about?"

The woman ambled over to the small hedge which separated the front garden from the road where Rose was standing.

"Oh, a man drowned, and they think that it might be our neighbour, Hendrich de Roo. We haven't heard anything more yet."

"Who is Hendrich de Roo, did he live here?"

"No, not up here in the actual community, but he had a little house, really a cottage, right down by the river. He was a scientist, I believe; kept himself to himself although he always waved at me as he walked by. It's such a shame."

"Did he leave his car parked up here and walk down to his property?"

"Oh, no, I don't think that he ever owned a car. I only ever saw him on foot."

"So, when did this tragedy happen?"

"Let me think, it was last Thursday, five days ago. Umm....are you the police or something because I've already given a statement to a nice officer."

Rose smiled, "Sorry, I've just got a very enquiring mind."

Susan interrupted her quickly, "Come on Rose, you've kept this good woman long enough." She extended her hand to the lady and continued, "Hi, I'm actually a retired detective and am also interested in what's going on here. I feel that you should know that Hendrich was murdered, and the police are seriously investigating this case. Where were you last Thursday if you don't mind me asking?"

"Well, as I told the officer who interviewed me, I was home as I mostly am these days. You see Bill, my husband, is on oxygen and can't leave the house so I'm here with him most of the time."

"Did you notice any cars parked on the road leading to the river?"

"Yes, there was one. A rather important looking man wearing a suit and carrying a briefcase got out and walked down the footpath towards Hendrich's place. Other than that, and of course Steve Wilson's van which is always here, he's our maintenance guy, it was just a regular quiet day."

"Thank you, Mrs... I'm so sorry, I didn't catch your name?"

"Oh, I'm Helen, Helen Burns, my hubby is Bill. Anytime you ladies need to chat, just knock on the door and you'd be welcomed."

"Thank you, Helen." Susan and Rose waved as they walked away.

"You haven't lost your touch, Susan." Rose said as they got into the car.

Susan laughed. "Well, I believe in the direct approach. Just say it as it is, is my motto. Now, when I get home, I'm going to call your handsome DCI and invite him over for dinner. Apart from wheedling information out of him, I need to check him out. Do you have his cell number?"

Rose nodded and drove off feeling a little cheated, not only Kate, but now Susan would enjoy the company of the only man, other than Tom, who had stirred her soul.

TWENTY

DC Brown drove while DC Elliot made hasty notes as they discussed what they would say during the upcoming interview of Barry Brown, CEO of Santé Industries. DC Brown agreed to be the bad cop in the good cop bad cop scenario, but only if Barry proved to be a hard nut to crack.

They pulled up outside a large, ultra-modern, and dazzling white modular building with smoked glass windows and angular roof lines. If outside appearances were anything to go by, then Santé appeared to be doing really well. DCI Hargreaves had called ahead and booked a time slot for the interview with the CEO so that when they arrived, they were shown almost immediately to Mr. Brown's office.

Barry Brown was in his early fifties, slightly paunchy, with silver hair, and a small goatee beard and moustache. His skin looked tanned and generally he had an air of good health, he probably played golf regularly and drank at the clubhouse liberally. He stood up from his desk when the two detectives entered the room.

"How can I help you, officers?"

He had a deep, smooth voice which resonated with authority. This was a man used to being in charge.

After introducing themselves and exchanging business cards DC Brown took the lead.

"We're here about the death of I believe, umm...a colleague of yours, Doctor Hendrich de Roo."

Barry looked momentarily shaken, "Did you say death? I only spoke to the man last week. May I ask how he died?"

"We are investigating a murder." DC. Brown pulled out of his pocket a folded sheet of paper cataloguing the dates and subject headings of all the emails sent to and from Hendrich and Barry.

"It appears that you have been in an ongoing communication with him constantly over the last six months. Some of these emails appear threatening in content."

Barry had sat down, and his previously tanned skin had now paled. He opened and closed his mouth like a fish as he gasped for words.

"Yes, well, umm...here's the thing, to be quite honest, officers, the man was a nut case. He kept going on about a miracle cure for all sorts of diseases. He even said that he had tested it on himself and that he was living proof that the drug worked. He was relentless in his pursuit, wanting us to run test trials ourselves to prove that his drug worked. The man was excessively annoying. We were contemplating taking legal action against him."

"Did you ever meet with him in person and give him a chance to show you his research?"

"Oh, no, no, we deal with crack pots like him almost daily. Believe me if I let in everyone claiming to have the miracle cure, I'd never get any work done around here. No, if you have read my emails then you will see that I tried to deal with him firmly, but fairly."

DC Elliot now took the lead. "Mr. Brown, where were you last Thursday around five-thirty?"

Barry paled even further as he spluttered, "You can't seriously suspect me of anything surely?"

"Just answer my question, sir."

"Umm... well, let me think. The office normally closes at five, unless there is a board meeting, but no, last Thursday it was straight home for me after work. I would have been on the 403 somewhere close to Hamilton where I live, by five-thirty."

"Can anyone corroborate that?"

"Well, my wife Jill can vouch for me I suppose. I would have been home by six at the latest."

"Right, if we could have her contact information, we'll have a word with her, and if it's alright with you we'll check with your secretary just in case you forgot something about last Thursday. Otherwise, we'll be in touch."

Barry showed the two officers to the door and afterwards he collapsed on his chair and put his head in his hands. Had he incriminated himself or, more to the point, his pharmaceutical company?

TWENTY-ONE

After Rose had dropped Susan off at her condo, she decided to call in on her sister, Kate.

She was greeted at the door by Lucy and the little kitten. Kate hugged her sister as she stepped into the hall.

"How nice to see you, can you stay for lunch? I'm just making myself a salad."

Rose looked at her watch and realized that it was actually lunch time. She had been out with Susan all morning and other than a muffin, she hadn't eaten anything since breakfast.

"Great, I'm starving; I'd love to stay for lunch but let me help you in the kitchen."

"Maybe you could set the table. We'll eat outside on the patio. It's such a beautiful day. So what's up, Rose?"

"Oh, not much, I've been hanging out with Susan this morning. Oh, by the way, she adores the kitten."

"Well, as you can see, she's not the only one in love with a kitten. Just look at Lucy, she's absolutely smitten."

Lucy and Fluffy were curled up on the sofa together, the kitten lying between the dog's paws just like a baby.

A few minutes later Kate carried out two plates laden with salad.

"I didn't have any cold cuts, so I've sliced up an avocado and some hard-boiled eggs. Oh, and I've got a lovely fresh baguette. Do you want a glass of wine?"

"Yes please," Rose said as she settled down on the patio chair appraising the fantastic work her sister had achieved in the garden. It was nothing short of a miracle how the back yard had been transformed into what looked like an English country garden.

When Kate had bought the cottage, the whole property had an air of neglect. Now there were shaped flower beds planted with petunias and pansies with a waterfall cascading into a small fishpond. Rocks surrounded the perimeter of the pool with various hostas and tall grasses planted strategically amongst the stone. The overall effect was charming.

When they were both settled and halfway through their lunch, Rose said nonchalantly, "So, how was your dinner date with DCI Hargreaves?"

Kate laughed or rather guffawed out aloud, "Oh, Rose, it was hardly a date. I just invited the man around for dinner more out of politeness than anything else. But, as you asked, I have to say we got on like a house on fire. He's so easy to talk to and, yes, I really do like him."

"Aha, do I sense romance in the air?" Rose said while sipping her wine and trying to sound as casual as she could.

Kate was quiet for a while and then answered her sister slowly. "You know something Rose, I don't really know if I'm ready yet for another relationship. I thought that I was, but I feel as if I'm running scared because John is not the sort to have just a casual affair. He's a serious guy and I would hate to break his heart."

"Well, you could just take it nice and slow and see where it goes. John seems like a decent guy, but there are plenty of other fish in the sea."

Kate laughed, "Yes, you're quite right. I'll see if he contacts me again and take it from there."

"Changing the subject somewhat, have you heard from Ally recently?"

"Funny you should ask that; we were on Facetime together yesterday. That reminds me, I need to let John know something. You know, Ally was devastated about Doctor de Roo's death.

"She remembered him telling her class all about a study he had been conducting where he had used himself as a guinea pig. The whole class thought that he was a bit crazy, but Ally said that he just wanted to prove his hypothesis and the only way that he could do that was to ingest some pathogens and wait for them to infect his internal organs.

"He then dosed himself with potassium metabisulfite. That was a couple of years ago, so he obviously lived to prove his hypothesis and then after all that he was murdered. What a tragedy."

"Give Ally my love next time you talk to her and tell her that Paul and Atsuko have just bought a little house, I'm sure that she'll be interested."

Ally and Paul had shared an apartment in London for one year when Paul had returned from Japan to work at Fanshawe College. The cousins had got on really well and had enjoyed their year together.

"So, how's work at the Albion going, Kate?"

Kate laughed again, "You know something, sis, I love it. I make loads of money off the tips, and I get to talk to great people, and I get paid to do all of that. What's there not to like?"

"Great, I'm really proud of you and so pleased that you're happy again. Now I really need to get back to the dogs. I've been out all morning and they'll be crossing their legs by now."

"Okay, but don't be a stranger. You and Tom must come around for drinks one evening. Maybe I'll invite Susan and possibly John. There, we have a plan."

TWENTY-TWO

The next day John arrived at the town hall just as a white van had pulled up in front of the building and was off loading a large box. A burly man in blue overalls ambled over to him.

"Are you in charge here, mate?"

"Umm... yes, and whom might you be?"

"We're from Serious Crimes in London, got a delivery for your incident room."

John now remembered that he had been notified that Headquarters would be sending them a SMART Board to use for the investigation. He had never used one before and muttered under his breath that it was a waste of valuable resources.

"Come this way, follow me, we're down in the basement, just be careful of the stairs."

The delivery man had just finished setting up the board when Constable Holly Ryan arrived. "Boy, I'm impressed, guv, fancy that, a SMART Board. I never thought I'd live to see the day that you embraced technology like this. Well done, guv."

"It was not my decision," John said stiffly, "I have no use for such a thing."

The rest of the team had all arrived and after the initial inspection and questions about the SMART Board, John finally got down to business.

"Right, good morning everyone, now let's get right down to our reports. Constables Brown and Elliot how did it go with Mr. Brown at the pharmaceutical company?"

Constable Brown shuffled some papers around and then proceeded to tell the team about their interview with Barry Brown. "He was definitely not telling us everything, sir, and seemed quite nervous and somewhat agitated. "

Constable Elliot piped up, "We did follow up with his secretary and his wife who assured us that he not only left the office at five that day but was home at his regular time of six. But they could of course be covering for him. However, we have a request in to the 407 ETR with his account details to verify his movements on Thursday"

"Thank you, Constables. Now, Sergeant Flowers, how was your trip to Manitoulin?"

Sergeant Flowers fished out his notebook and began to read, "I managed to charter a flight into Gore Airport, a really tiny airport if ever there was one, and I was met by the local OPP who drove me to Meldrum Bay. I met with Mrs. de Roo yesterday and she told me that Rose Blair had already been to see her and had asked after her son. However, Mrs. Blair had not told her that her son was dead. She was obviously very distraught to hear that he had been murdered. Her son, apparently, had been obsessed with the Bayfield River. He had told her how he had discovered all sorts of nasty protozoa in the water."

Constable Ryan interrupted him, "What are protozoa?"

"Protozoa are basically parasites, part of the pathogens found in river water. Hendrich had apparently written a number of research papers on this subject. Mrs. de Roo said that he had phoned her last year and was so excited that he could barely speak.

"Apparently, he had conducted an experiment on himself and claimed that he had found a cure for a number of water-borne diseases. She went on to say that he had contacted Santé, one of the biggest pharmaceutical companies in Ontario and that they had apparently rejected him outright.

"She also said that he hadn't phoned or emailed her for a number of weeks which wasn't particularly unusual as when he was focused on his work everything went by the wayside. It does tell us, sir, that our victim did have a phone. His mother said that he bought a new smart phone a few years ago at her insistence because, after his dad died, she felt the need to be in touch with him more often. That's about all I've got, sir."

"Thank you, Sergeant. I suspected that he would have had a phone, but we haven't found one yet and the SOC team and forensics have combed the area thoroughly. Right, Constable Ryan, did you find any red flags on his computer? "

Holly stood up and brought her laptop over to the Smart board, she then tapped on the keyboard. There, on the large white screen appeared emails from Hendrich's computer.

"So, guv, I've highlighted the emails of interest. As you can see there are dozens from Santé, which we've already discussed, a few from Doctor Cave, and some from his mom, but this one I found interesting. It's not actually an email but Doctor de Roo had googled Vanastra. Look, I'll pull up what came up on his Google search."

On the screen, headlined in bold was CFB Clinton and the proceeding article talked about a top-secret British Commonwealth Air Training unit for radio operatives.

In July 1943, the Range and Direction Finding (RDF) School was decommissioned and the Royal Canadian Air Force (RCAF) No.5 Radio School was created. In June 1944 the Radio School was transferred to the RCAF's Home War Operatives Training Command.

By the end of the Second World War in November 1945, the RCAF Station in Clinton became home to a Radar and Communications School.

In February 1963 the RCAF merged with the Royal Canadian Navy and the Royal Canadian Armed Forces resulting in RCAF Clinton changing its name to Canadian Forces Base, Clinton, CFB Clinton.

The base was finally closed in 1971 and the buildings were sold off to a real estate developer. It is now known as the village of Vanastra, Ontario.

The team read the article and then sat in silence while they waited for DCI Hargreaves to continue.

"Hmm...well, very interesting, but I cannot see the relevance to our investigation, Holly? Why would Hendrich de Roo bother to Google Vanastra? Constable, did you find anything else of significance in your email search that is connected to this information?"

"Not really, guv, apart from several emails from Doctor Cave where she talks about ground water sources and the Bayfield River."

"I spent last night reading through many of the research papers written by the doctor and a couple of collaborative ones written with Doctor Cave. They proved difficult reading, but the gist of them was to do with the five groups of pathogens and in particularly, protozoa and helminths. In layman terms, we're talking about parasites in our water sources and, in this case, in the Bayfield River. Doctor Cave is studying contaminants in the ground water. Her specific area of interest is quite local in as much as she is studying contaminant seepage in the Clinton-Bayfield area. It still eludes me how any of this connects to our case?"

Constable Holly put up her hand, "Guv, I'm going to put up a map of this Clinton, Bayfield area on the SMART Board."

She tapped on her laptop and soon an enlarged map of the area popped up on the screen. John walked over to the board and pointed out Vanastra and then followed with his finger where the Bayfield River geographically flowed in relation to it.

"It's quite some distance and as far as I can see Vanastra is between the Maitland River and the Bayfield River. No, I cannot see how this can be at all relevant to our case. So, let me summarize what we do know, the facts as we have them. We do know that Santé Industries was feeling antagonized by Hendrich de Roo's persistent emails. Could Barry Brown have met with the doctor, got into an argument, and then hit him on the head with the log? Right now, that seems to be the only possible explanation. We're still waiting for the DNA results taken from the log, hopefully we'll have them tomorrow. I think that I'll pay Barry a visit myself and take a DNA sampling kit with me. Any further thoughts?"

Sergeant Flowers put up his hand. "Sir, I would like to speak to Doctor Cave once more. It seems that she was the closest to Hendrich and as such might be privy to much more information about the man, both private and academic."

"Yes, you're right, Sergeant, we don't really know much

about him, do we? Do you want to interview her here or in London?"

"I think that it's better if I go to the university and talk to her there on her own territory. If I think that she's hiding anything or being at all evasive, then we can get her over here."

"Good thinking, Sergeant, but also ask around the department and see what the other academics thought of both Doctors Hendrich and Cave.

"Right, so Constables Brown and Elliot, I would like you to drive out to Vanastra and talk to a few people and generally get the lay of the land out there.

"Constable Holly keep trolling through all those emails and see if anything else leaps out at you. Okay, we'll meet again tomorrow."

They were about to leave when John's phone vibrated.

"DCI Hargreaves speaking."

It was Susan Parker, John covered the phone with his hand and waved to his team mouthing that he would see them all the next day, he then went back to the phone. After introducing herself, Susan proceeded to invite John around for dinner that evening. John looked at his watch, it was only one o'clock, he could type up his reports and still have time to drive to Brampton and back, but dinner would have to be later, more like seven than six.

When he relayed that information to Susan she laughed. "Oh, in Italy we never ate dinner before nine or even ten at night. I still haven't got used to our Canadian ways of eating so early. Let's make dinner for eight o'clock. That way you won't be rushing."

Having agreed on a time they said their goodbyes leaving John to muse about his good fortune. He would finally get to meet the iconic DCI Susan Parker in person. He had heard so much about her at Headquarters where she was something of a legend.

TWENTY-THREE

Rose spent the afternoon going over what she and Susan had found out about the death of Hendrich de Roo. She had made a phone call to Lora in Manitoulin to offer her condolences, but also to ask her a few questions.

"Lora, did Hendrich have a girlfriend?"

"No, well not as far as I know, but you do have to realize how private he was. I'm sure I would have known if there had been a relationship in the wind. There was a female post-graduate student who he was advising, and I also think that they were co-writing some research papers together. That's the only female I can remember him mentioning. To be honest, Rose, he was so absorbed in his work, he really didn't have time for anything or anyone else."

"One more thing, Lora, did your son have any enemies?"

Lora gasped, "No, no, he was a quiet, kind man who kept himself to himself. I suppose a fellow academic might have been jealous of his success, but that wouldn't have bothered Hendrich. He wasn't competitive; he was concerned that mankind was destroying the planet with awful pollutants and so he made it his life's work to understand pathogens and their effect on the environment.

He was always going on about farmers and the fertilizers and pesticides they used. Our water, he used to say, was a precious commodity and we were all stewards of this earth and we needed to take care of our assets. Hendrich was passionate about conservation."

"Thank you, Lora. Your son sounded like a wonderful scientist. Listen, I'm doing some digging and I promise that I'll do everything I can to find out who murdered Hendrich. I'm sure that the police are also doing all they can too. I'll phone you next week, but please let me know when the funeral is to be held so that Tom and I can attend, if that's okay by you?"

"Oh, Rose, of course you must come to the funeral, but they haven't released his body yet so it might not be for another few weeks, I'll be sure to let you know as soon as I have a date. Thanks, my dear for everything."

Rose put the phone down and went over to put the kettle on. She needed to write down everything that she had learnt from Lora although it wasn't really much to go on. One bit of information had given her pause for thought, the fact that his post-graduate student was also female.

In Rose's experience men rarely spent a lifetime being celibate, unless of course one was a priest.

Hendrich would have been no exception and even though he had been totally wrapped up in his work he would still have had normal manly desires and needs. If, and of course this was purely hypothetical, he had become romantically involved with his graduate student, then it could be quite possible that they might have had a lover's tiff and, in a rage, she had bumped him off; a crime of passion.

Maybe I've been watching too much Netflix, Rose thought as she grabbed a notebook and started making a list of the facts that she and Susan actually knew, not far-flung fantasies based on the dramatic.

The first undeniable fact that he had been found down river from his house with his head smashed in, was indisputable as was the estimated time of death.

Second, his academic work was all consuming; he had been obsessed with trying to get a proper drug trial conducted through the reputable pharmaceutical company known as Santé. Could this obsession have led to his death?

Rose's gut feeling said that whilst being continually pestered by the scientist no pharmaceutical company would go to the extreme of silencing the man for good. No, the femme fatal in the guise of the post-graduate student seemed more likely.

Rose made a mental note to call Susan to make sure that when she had John around for dinner that she grilled him about the student.

Looking at her notes Rose realized just how little they knew about Hendrich de Roo. She let out a deep sigh as she made a pot of tea and went to sit in the sunroom with Puff and Ben. It was time to do some serious thinking.

SUSAN WAS ALSO in deep thought over at Harbour Court. She had prepared two large steaks and had made a big salad, well, she had bought a store made salad and dumped the contents into a bowl and chopped up some tomatoes to scatter on top. A tub of store-bought potato salad sat in the fridge alongside an apple pie from Zehrs Country market.

Susan rarely cooked. Barbecuing was usually the closest

that she ever came to being a cook. But still, it was summer and what could be nicer and more delicious than two juicy steaks cooked to perfection on the grill, eaten outside and washed down with beer and wine. Her reverie was broken by Rose calling her and sounding slightly manic.

"Susan, when you see John, umm...I mean DCI Hargreaves, you must ask him about a post-graduate student. Lora, Hendrich's mom, mentioned her to me when I was speaking to her. I feel that she might be the key to the murder investigation, and I also think that maybe she was having an affair with Hendrich..."

"Slow down, Rose. Right, well, I do have John coming around later for dinner and yes, I will ask him about this woman. Leave it to me, I'll squeeze every tiny bit of information out of him."

Rose experienced a flash of jealousy streak through her, but she quickly put it to one side. Thanking Susan, she put down the phone and went into the kitchen to start preparing their dinner. That night they would be eating chicken and mushroom pie, sauté potatoes with cauliflower au-gratin, and for dessert an apple crumble and whipped cream: Tom's favourite pudding.

TWENTY-FOUR

John glanced at his watch. It was five o'clock and the traffic on the 403 was backing up horribly. He would be hard pushed to get back to Bayfield by seven o'clock and felt relieved that Susan had set a later dinner time than normal. An Audi cut in front of him and then proceeded to weave in and out of the traffic like a possessed demon. *Bloody Toronto drivers,* John thought as he braked hard and tried to ease himself out of the fast lane. The whole afternoon had really been a bit of a waste of time, although he had managed to get a DNA sample off Barry Brown with very little hassle which had surprised him. Suspects, when asked if they would allow a DNA test, usually resisted. Barry had just looked surprised, but had said, "Sure, why not, if it will eliminate me from your murder enquiry go ahead."

John had not got any more useful information from the interview. The man was a prize jerk, that was one thing for certain, and the tone of his emails to Hendrich had been totally aggressive, but he hadn't broken any laws and so they had very little to hold against him. John did at least have his

DNA sample which could now be compared to the DNA found on the murder weapon.

He arrived at Susan's just after seven twenty having driven straight over to her place without stopping to change and he was now regretting his rush.

Catching a glimpse of himself in the hall mirror, John thought that he looked decidedly crumpled and wished that he had at least changed his shirt. Susan greeted him warmly, European style with a kiss on each cheek. She looked stunning in a plain turquoise blue sheath dress with matching earrings and a pendant necklace. Her feet were clad in strappy Italian sandals and her arms tinkled with multiple bracelets.

"Welcome, umm... John, you don't mind me calling you John, do you?"

John laughed and immediately the ice was broken.

"I do hope that you like barbeques because that's all I can cook. I've got us some lovely steaks. I'll put them on now as I'm sure that you're starving."

John felt his stomach grumble, he had stopped on his way up to Brampton at a service station and had bought a tasteless chicken wrap and coffee, but that was hours ago. A juicy steak would be just the ticket, he thought as he followed Susan out on to her small courtyard of a garden which was mostly taken up with a large hot tub.

John lifted the lid up and looked inside. "My daughter has one of these and you know something, I've never been in it. Do you use yours much?"

Susan smiled and said, "It was my retirement present to myself and yes, I go in at least once a day, it's so relaxing. I do some of my best thinking in the hot-tub."

They spent the rest of the evening chatting and soon felt very comfortable in each other's company. Susan finally got around to asking him about his current murder investigation. It appeared that John was at first unwilling to discuss the case with her until she pointed out that it had only been a couple of years since she had been investigating a murder and as two professionals, she felt that her input might prove valuable to him.

"Well, put it that way how can I resist. Now, what do you want to know?"

By the end of the evening Susan had been bought up to speed on the whole investigation and John left her condo feeling that he had made a new and like- minded friend in Bayfield.

TWENTY-FIVE

The next day with the entire team assembled at the Town Hall, John shared the full forensics report from the pathology lab in Toronto. According to the report Hendrich de Roo had extremely high levels of PCBs in his blood, his liver was totally shot through with cancerous cells, non-Hodgkin's lymphoma and malignant melanomas had coursed through his body. The man had been lucky to have still been alive before he was murdered.

Sergeant Flowers put up his hand. "Sir, when I interviewed Doctor Cave again, she talked about PCBs in her ground water research, I wonder if there's a connection?"

"Thank you, Sergeant, we'll come back to your report later, but for now I want to read out the DNA results which have just come through. It appears that our murderer did not wear gloves as there are very clear DNA markers on one end of the log. Not surprisingly Hendrich de Roo's DNA was extracted from the other end from the traces of brain matter, skin, and hair from his scalp. They ran the DNA results through the database of known DNAs, and nothing popped up which is not surprising really as, unless our murderer has a criminal record, it would not be in our system."

Constable Holly put her hand up, "Can the DNA results determine the sex of the perpetrator, guv?"

John nodded his head. "Yes, there is a marker in DNA that determines the sex and ethnic origins. You'll be surprised to learn that markers indicated our DNA contains both male and female markers, both Caucasian."

"How could there be both, guv? Surely two people couldn't have killed him?"

"No, two people couldn't have killed him, but two people could have handled the murder weapon. As a matter of interest, Holly, did you have anyone in mind for the female DNA handler?"

Holly looked unsure. "Well, the only female we've interviewed in this investigation is Doctor Cave and she was very familiar with him and very ambitious. I had wondered if they might have been involved in a romantic relationship?"

"That could be a possibility, but we still don't have a motive for murder?"

"Yeah, well I hadn't worked that one out either, guv."

"Okay, so let's get back to our reports. Sergeant, fill us in with your interview and what you learnt about PCBs."

Sergeant Flowers stood up and pulled out his notepad. "I haven't typed this up yet, sir, but I will later today. Right, I have to say that throughout the interview I felt as if I was being lectured to like a student. Doctor Cave is passionate about her research work, particularly the paper she was collaborating on with Hendrich de Roo.

"Whereas his work focused on pathogens, her research was primarily to do with contaminants in ground water sources which leech their way into the rivers and lakes. She studies invertebrates, mostly mud feeders like salamanders, newts, and tiny fish and apparently, any toxicity in the water can be discovered by studying the vertebrates or in other words, the fish skeletons."

John interrupted his sergeant. "That's all very interesting, but how exactly can this be connected to our inquiry?"

"I'm getting to that, sir, according to results collected over a two-year period, analysing invertebrates and tracking the level of toxicity, the conclusion is that there is an extremely high level of PCB contaminants in the Bayfield River, particularly upriver from Hendrich's cottage."

Constable Brown put up his hand, "I know that this sounds ignorant, but what exactly are PCBs?"

John shot Sergeant Flowers a glance and said, "Okay, Sergeant, now it's your chance to explain what PCBs are to all of us, go ahead and give us a lecture."

Sergeant Flowers cleared his throat before beginning to talk. "PCB, which is an acronym for Polychlorinated biphenyl, is an organic chlorine compound once widely deployed as dielectric and coolant fluids in electrical apparatus, carbonless copy paper, and in heat transfer fluids. Because of their longevity, PCBs are still widely in use, even though their manufacture has declined drastically since the 1960s, when a host of problems associated with their extreme toxicity to humans were identified.

"With their classification as a persistent organic pollutant, their production was banned by United States by federal law in 1978 and by the Stockholm Convention on Persistent Organic Pollutants in 2001.

"According to Wikipedia, the International Agency for Research on Cancer rendered PCBs as definite carcinogens in humans. According to the U.S. Environmental Protection

Agency, PCBs cause cancer in animals and are probable human carcinogens.

"Many rivers and buildings, including schools, parks, and other sites, are still contaminated with PCBs and there has been contamination of food supplies with the substances. Some PCBs share a structural similarity and toxic mode of action with dioxins. Other toxic effects such as endocrine disruption and neurotoxicity are known.

"The maximum allowable contaminant level in drinking water in Canada and the United States is set at zero, but because of the limitations of water treatment technologies, a level of 0.5 parts per billion is the de facto level.

"Fish who make up the largest of the vertebrates, have been swimming in earth's water for over five million years, and are particularly susceptible to ingesting even the smallest quantities of PCBs which is why microbiologists study them to determine toxicity in water. Any questions?"

Constable Holly said, "Yeah, but how does this all tie in with our murder?"

"Doctor Cave and Doctor de Roo thought that from water sampling in the Bayfield River, they had discovered a source of ground water contamination and as far as Doctor Cave was aware, Hendrich had every intention of confronting the landowner. Maybe he did just that and a fight ensued, I don't know, but that could be one possible explanation."

"Thank you, Sergeant. Did you get to talk to any of the other department staff at the university?"

"Oh, yes I did and there was a mixed reaction to both our doctors. Hendrich was very well respected, but considered a strange, reclusive guy, whereas Doctor Cave generally was considered both pushy and aggressive and not very well liked. It appears that she saw a lot of Hendrich and there were rumours going around the department that they were in a relationship together, but that was pure office gossip, sir."

"Thank you, Sergeant, you did well and that has certainly given us much to think about. We will have to investigate further the source of this contamination although it sounds more like an environmental task than actual police work. I think that I'll have another talk with Doctor Cave before involving the Ministry of Environment. Constables Brown and Elliot, what information did you discover about Vanastra?"

Constable Brown stood up and pulled out his notebook. "Right, well, as Holly has previously told us, the RAF Radar Training School was established in July 1941 by the Canadian Royal Air Force under the British Commonwealth Air Training Plan. After the war, unlike many RCAF stations, Clinton was not closed down, it became an Air Radar Office School, School for Food Services, and the Aerospace Engineering Officers School.

"In 1971, the base was closed and sold to real estate developer John Van Gastel, who changed the name to Vanastra. When the military base was decommissioned, all the large radar equipment was removed by the RCAF, but the office equipment and general electrical items were taken away by a contractor to be disposed of accordingly."

John interrupted his Constable, "Who was the contractor and what did he do with all the equipment?"

"Oh, I can find no records of the contractor although one elderly man told me that the contractor was a local. Of course, this happened over forty years ago, sir."

"Right, well, we do need to find out the name of the contractor, thank you, Constable. So, in summary, let's see what we've got. Our prime suspect is still Barry Brown of

Santé Industries although my instinct is beginning to rule him out.

He offered up his DNA without any hesitation, not the actions of a guilty man, however, his emails to the diseased were particularly vicious. We will have to wait for the DNA results. Just suppose for now that Hendrick de Roo was about to reveal the source of the ground water contamination. How would the owner of the land leaching the toxic waste, react? I should imagine the Ministry of Environment levies extremely large penalties to anyone dumping or spilling toxic waste material.

"We do need to get Doctor Cave back in here and ask her directly where Hendrich and she had pinpointed the source of the contamination. I'll telephone her and suggest that she comes here tomorrow morning."

Sergeant Flowers frowned. "She won't like that sir. I think that she's lecturing all this week."

"Well then she will just have to reschedule. This is a murder inquiry not a university debate. Right, drinks are on me at The Albion. Good work, team. I think that we're finally making some progress."

TWENTY-SIX

Susan and Rose had met that morning over coffee and scones; Susan relayed to Rose all the information that she had preened from John Hargreaves during the course of their dinner together the previous evening.

"So, you see Rose, they still have very little to go on other than those nasty emails from Barry Brown of Santé Industries."

"Oh, I don't know, Susan, I reckon that Dr Cave knows much more than she's letting on. You don't work so closely with someone without forming some kind of a relationship.

"So, let's look at the facts: she was co-writing a research paper with Hendrich on Ground Water Contamination in the Bayfield River. Did they find much in the way of contamination in the river? Was that why Hendrich's organs were so fried? Didn't you say that his body had also been sent to forensics in Toronto for further analysis?

"I remember Lora, his mom, saying something about him using his own body as a guinea pig to find a cure for pathogenic toxins. So where does all this lead us, and why would someone kill him over something like water contamination?"

"Slow down, Rose, you're jumping to conclusions too fast. Yes, I agree with you about Dr Cave; I think that we should maybe go and have a friendly chat with her."

Susan looked at her watch and saw that it was almost lunch time. She had arranged to have a drink with John at The Little Inn that evening but, if they left right away, they could drive to London and still be back by early evening.

"So, Rose, should we go to London right now? There's no time like the present and I really want to get to grips with this whole water thing."

Rose smiled and said, "A girl after my own heart. Yes, I'll leave a note for Tom. I've already prepared dinner so that's okay. Let's do it. I'm ready whenever you are."

The two friends got into Susan's car. She had bought herself the silver Porsche two years ago as a retirement present and drove it like a Formula 1 driver.

They drove to London in record time with Rose clutching the inside door handle for the whole duration of the journey. She found Susan's driving terrifying.

Pulling into the car park at Western University they spent the next half an hour tracking down the microbiology department. Finally, they found it and Dr Cave's office.

"You take the lead, Rose," Susan said, although as it turned out it was Susan herself who ended up taking the lead.

They knocked on Dr. Cave's door and were greeted by a fresh-faced young woman wearing blue jeans and a white t-shirt.

"Oh, can I help you?"

"Umm... we're looking for Dr Cave," Rose said wondering if she was actually talking to the Doctor.

"Do you have an appointment? Dr Cave never mentioned anything about visitors. I'm her assistant. Is there anything I can help you with?"

"Well, we really wanted to speak to Dr Cave herself, is she in? We don't mind waiting if she could see us soon?"

"Oh, no, Dr Cave left for Bayfield over an hour ago. I'll tell her that you called. What are your names?"

Susan stepped forward and pulled out her old Police card which she had forgotten to hand in after she had retired. "That won't be necessary. I'm DCI Parker and this is my assistant, Ms. Blair. It is urgent that we contact Dr Cave as part of an ongoing murder enquiry."

"But an officer was only here yesterday talking to Doctor Cave, is everything alright?"

"No, put it this way, Dr Cave has some very valuable information and it's imperative that we find her."

"Is there anything I can help you with? I've worked alongside Dr Cave this past year. I might be able to answer some of your questions?"

"Did Doctor Cave ever mention locating a source of contaminated ground water in the Bayfield River? We know from our investigations that Dr de Roo and Dr Cave were close to revealing the site and we are anxious to contact the owner as he might be able to help us with our investigation."

"I'll show you something." The young assistant walked over to the wall where a large map had been taped, and a big circle had been drawn on the map.

"This is a map of the Bayfield and Clinton area. If you look at the circled area you will see the Bayfield River, Dr de Roo's cottage, and over here is the community of Vanastra. This large black mark is at the estimated location of the source of the ground water contamination. This here," she pointed west of the circled area, "Is where the Holmesville dump is located, but it is now closed. Initially Dr Cave thought that there had been leeching from the dump, but Dr de Roo disproved her theory as any seepage would have migrated into the Maitland River, not The Bayfield River. No, it looks like this area," she said pointing to a location on Parr Line close to the Bayfield River, "is the most likely source."

Susan and Rose studied the map carefully. Susan took out her phone and took a photograph of it. She turned to Dr Cave's helpful assistant.

"Do you have Dr Cave's cell number?"

The assistant shook her head. "I've already tried calling her. I suspect that she's left her phone behind somewhere. I'm afraid that she's very absent minded and it's not at all uncommon for her to forget her phone."

"Okay, well, thank you, hopefully we'll be able to make contact with her sooner rather than later."

When they were outside of the office Rose said, "You were brilliant, Susan, but aren't you breaking the law saying that you're a DCI and showing her your old warrant card.?"

Susan laughed, "Technically, I haven't told any lies, just omitted to say that I am now a retired police officer. No harm done."

"Oh well if you're not bothered, then I'm okay. But it does look like we've missed the boat with Dr Cave."

Susan shook her head. "No, I reckon if we were to head over to Parr Line right now, we'd stand a good chance of finding Dr Cave. Just wait here while I pop back into the office and ask her assistant what kind of car she drives."

Susan was back a few minutes later. "She drives a bright red Toyota Prius. That should be easy to spot. Let's go and catch us a professor."

TWENTY-SEVEN

Back in Bayfield DCI Hargreaves and his team were enjoying a late lunch washed down by a few beers. Kate was serving at the bar when John went to place the order.

"Oh good, I was hoping to see you here, Kate. I wanted to say thank you so much for a lovely meal last night and wanted to know if you would join me for dinner at The Little Inn sometime later this week? When are you free?"

Kate beamed. "Oh, John, how lovely, let me see, I'm free tomorrow night if that works and I would love to have dinner with you."

"Right, that's a deal, I'll pick you up at seven then."

"Oh, that's silly I'll walk over and join you at The Little Inn. I could do with the exercise."

"That's great. I'll see you tomorrow."

He paid for their drinks and lunch and walked back to his team with a big smile on his face.

"You look like the cat's pyjamas, guv, is that your girlfriend?"

John tapped his nose, but smiled as he said, "She's a friend, Holly, just a friend."

"That's what they all say, guv." Holly laughed and her eyes twinkled.

Just then Tom and his golfing buddies, Gary and Peter, arrived. John waved them over.

"Hey, Tom, how are things? I haven't seen you or your lady wife for a while?"

Tom smiled. He had popped back home after golf and had found Rose's note saying that she had gone to London with Susan to meet up with a Dr Cave from the university. He told John what Rose and Susan were up to and was surprised by his reaction.

"That's funny as I just phoned Dr Cave's office and her assistant said that she was out all day and had come to Bayfield. It looks like Rose and Susan have had an abortive journey."

Tom laughed, "Well, if you know Rose you would also know that she's like a dog with an old bone when she gets a whiff of a murder. No excuses, John, but I know my wife and she'll be solving your murder sooner rather than later."

John remembered the previous year when Rose had followed an ambulance which was the hiding place for the murderer of Windmill Lake. If she hadn't had tracked the ambulance down, they would have lost the chase. Yes, she was a formidable woman, but a danger to herself and others getting involved with police work.

"Well, I'd rather she didn't poke her nose into our investigation, Tom. It worries me as we could be dealing with some desperate people."

Tom sighed, "I know, John, I know. I've told her a dozen times to butt out and I'm afraid she doesn't listen, never has. At least she has Susan Parker with her this time and she of all people should know what she's doing. No, the two of them together are both capable women; I'm not worried about them, so you shouldn't be either."

John shook his head and sighed, "Right, if you're not concerned then I'm okay so long as she lets us know if she finds something out. I'll try to be cool about it. Why don't you join us for drinks?"

Tom, Peter, and Gary pulled up some chairs and joined in the conversation and soon great guffaws of laughter could be heard in the bar at the Albion.

TWENTY-EIGHT

Susan and Rose were just approaching Lucan when Rose said in a small voice, "You know, Susan, I think we're going on a wild goose chase trying to track down Doctor Cave like this. Look let's stop off here at Tim Horton's and review the situation. Apart from anything else, I'm starving."

Susan pulled into the Tim Horton's.

"Right, we'll discuss it over lunch, but you do realize that any hope of catching her will go out of the window if we stop here too long."

"But that's exactly what I'm saying," Rose said earnestly, "Trying to catch up to her is rather bizarre, don't you think? We can wait until tomorrow to speak to her and still get the answers that we're looking for. No, I say that if we do anything today it would be to try to determine the source of the ground water contamination.

"We have the map and there aren't many farms or landowners in that circled area. We could also try to locate the drainage site of the ground water into the river," Rose was interrupted mid-sentence by her cell phone ringing. It was Anne, her daughter phoning from Ryerson in Toronto.

"Oh, hi, Mom, I wanted to let you know that I don't think that we're going to come down to Bayfield this weekend."

"Oh darling, that's a shame. Your father and I were so looking forward to seeing you all again. Why can't you come?"

There was a slight pause before Anne spoke.

"Actually, Mom, Allan and I are splitting up. I've spoken to a lawyer and she's drawing up a separation agreement."

"Oh darling, that's awful. What's happened?"

There was a loud sob on the other end of the line and then Anne continued, "Oh, Mom, he's been cheating on me. I can barely believe it myself."

"But how, I mean I thought that he was looking after the children. When would he have found the time? Anne, are you sure?"

"Of course I'm sure. If you have to know the sordid details, he met her at the toddler's group he takes the kids to. She's a nanny of all things and she's so beautiful and she's only twenty-three. Honestly, Mom, I'm through with him."

"Oh darling, I'm so terribly sorry. Can your father and I do anything?"

"I'm not sure. I'm trying to get an au pair or nanny right now. I've chucked Allan out and put the kids into the university day care, but it's horribly expensive. I'll let you know my plans when I know them myself."

"My love, I'm so sorry, look I'll phone you this evening. Love you darling."

Rose put her phone down and turned to Susan. "And so it begins, Tom and I knew that things were not going well between them, but I never thought that Greg would be the cheating kind."

"Oh, you are so naïve, Rose. He's a man." Susan said with a snigger.

"I know, I know. Oh well, let's have some lunch, there is nothing I can do right now."

Over lunch they talked about the case with Rose laying bets on Doctor Cave being somehow involved in the murder.

"But what would have been her motive, Rose?" Susan said while chomping her way through a BLT wrap. "Unless it was something to do with her position at the university? You know how difficult it is to get tenure. Maybe Hendrich wouldn't support her for whatever reason? Oh God, Rose, this is all pure speculation."

"I know, Susan, but I quite like your theory, although I'm still gambling on the woman scorned angle or woman rejected, it probably has nothing to do with any of that. What about the ground water contamination theory? Or, for that matter the CEO of Santé pharmaceuticals? I say that we're still a long way from having this case solved, don't you?"

"Come on you negative Nancy, eat up, we've got some farms to visit and people to talk to. "

Soon the two women were back on the road again heading towards Varna and Parr Line.

TWENTY-NINE

After John left the Albion, he decided to drive out to look at Vanastra himself. He had been interested to hear all about the old Radar School and intrigued by the role it had played in the Second World War.

Who would have thought that a small village on the edge of Clinton would have played such a pivotal part in the war? Quite amazing really, he mused as he drove along crossing the temporary bridge spanning the Bayfield River.

He wondered if Doctor Cave would contact him as she was supposed to be in the area and for that matter, what was she doing back in Bayfield? Maybe he should stop off at the murder victim's cottage and review the scene of the crime and generally have another nose around.

Even though the CSI teams and Forensics had thoroughly combed the area, it never ceased to amaze John what could be missed in a search and found later.

Hendrich's telephone was still missing and in all likelihood was sitting at the bottom of the river by now, but John was ever hopeful that someone would find it and hopefully that someone might be him. Looking at a crime scene with fresh eyes could often reveal new information.

John looked back from The Docks to where the new bridge was taking place. The young construction worker, Ryan, who had found the body, had been both articulate and very sensible when interviewed and John had taken an instant shine to him. We could do with bright, young men like that in the police force, he thought and wondered whether he should seek Ryan out and try to recruit him. Maybe at the end of the investigation he might do just that.

Turning right onto Old River Road he drove up the hill through a tunnel of trees until he reached Carriage Lane which was a comparatively new sub-division of beautiful and large modern houses.

At the end of the lane, he turned right on to the Bayfield River Road, passed the entrance to the Bayfield River Road Brewery, then Orchard Line on the left, and before he knew it was at The Happy Valley Adult Community.

John parked his car at the top of the bluff and got out. He was about to walk down the embankment when he noticed a woman working in her small front garden and a man sitting in a wheelchair, a clear plastic tube running from his nose into a small oxygen tank hooked to the side of his chair.

The woman stopped what she was doing and greeted John. "Hi there, more police I assume. I only spoke to your lot yesterday; how can I help you?"

John wondered who it was that she had spoken to, as Constables Brown and Elliot had interviewed the whole community the day after the murder and that was almost a week ago. He let that go for the moment and introduced himself.

"I'm DCI Hargreaves."

"Well, I'm Helen and this is my husband, Bill. Have you caught the murderer?

"No, but we've got a few good leads. Now, Helen if you can cast your mind back to last Thursday, I believe you said that the only visitor Dr de Roo had was in the afternoon. Did you know who this visitor was?"

"Well, I've never seen him before, but he looked like a businessman. He didn't stay long, barely ten minutes, oh, and he was carrying a brief case with him."

"Could you describe him to me, please."

"Let me think about it, yes, he was probably in his fifties, somewhat paunchy, grey silver hair, oh, he had a goatee, and wore a grey suit which seemed odd for a summer's day. Bill, did you see him? Maybe you could tell the officer what car he was driving as I'm hopeless with makes of cars."

Bill, who had been listening to the conversation, loudly spoke up with a deep gravelly voice.

"I don't know about the man Helen saw, but there has been a bright red Toyota Prius parked behind our house on and off for the past couple of months. I noticed it way back in April. I know my cars you see officer and I was particularly interested in this one as it's a part electric and part gas model, a hybrid car with great fuel consumption."

"That's very interesting. Did you ever see the owner of the car?"

"Yeah well, not that I was snooping or anything, but I was intrigued you see, anyway, yes, it was a young thing, the driver I mean, maybe in her twenties or early thirties with long blond hair worn back in a ponytail. She was quite petite and a looker too if you know what I mean. I reckon that the doctor and she were up to some hanky-panky, if you ask me that is."

Helen was looking at Bill with daggers in her eyes. John quickly intervened. "Thank you, Bill, you've been most helpful, now, were there any more visitors that day?"

Helen glanced at Bill and then said, "Umm... not that I can remember. What about you Bill? Anymore pretty young things?"

Bill just laughed. "The only other person hanging around that day was Steve, our maintenance guy. His pick-up was there like it is most afternoons, although he's not here today I see."

John looked up from his notebook, "So this Steve spends a lot of time here, does he?"

"Oh yes, he's our go-to person, we all use him if anything goes wrong or needs fixing. He also cleans the gutters and blows the leaves in the fall and the snow in the winter. He has a small contracting business."

"Where does Steve live?"

Helen turned to Bill and said, "Love, where does Steve live?"

"I'm not deaf, love, I heard the officer. I think that he lives on a farm somewhere down Parr Line or around there anyway."

"And what is the name of his business?"

"Oh, didn't I tell you? It's Wilson's Contractors, I believe it was his dad's business before he took it over. He used to build houses, but that's all in the past now."

John snapped his notebook closed and thanked Helen and Bill. He walked down the embankment deep in thought, three things had leapt out at him immediately: first, why had Doctor Cave failed to mention her brief visit to Dr. de Roo on that fatal Thursday, and second, why had no one mentioned that

Steve the contractor had been on site the afternoon of the murder? And then the description that matched Barry Brown from Santé Industries, what on earth was he doing visiting Hendrich? *This new information could be the breakthrough we need in this investigation,* he thought.

THIRTY

Doctor Deb Cave had left London that morning with the sole intention of finding Wilson Contractors on Parr Line. She had Googled the name and found an actual address. The big decision was whether to telephone beforehand or to just turn up unannounced. She knew if she pre-empted her arrival the contractor could quite easily make himself scarce and so she chose the latter and that was to arrive unannounced.

The journey to Parr Line, at least until Varna, was uneventful. It was another beautiful day with a clear blue sky and a perfect temperature of twenty-two degrees. Deb decided to stop at the Stonehouse Brewery. She needed a bit of Dutch courage to see her through the ensuing confrontation.

The Stonehouse Brewery had opened four years ago and was doing really well. They specialized in a Czech Pilsner which Deb loved. She ordered her beer and took it to an outside table where she sipped the brew while contemplating what she would say to the contractor.

She knew that he would flatly deny all knowledge of

taking and disposing of the electrical materials from Vanastra, but she held a trump card up her sleeve. She had managed to lay her hands on a manifesto document with the inventory of the items removed by Wilson's Contractor. The sticking point would be finding out exactly where the items had been disposed of on his property. Once the Ministry of the Environment got involved, they would dig up his whole property if necessary if he refused to play ball.

A small voice inside Deb's head was urging her to not involve herself, but just to contact the Ministry and let them deal with the issue. She had, however spent years on this ground water research project and it seemed almost churlish now not to see it through to its final conclusion. Deb also knew what Hendrich would have done; he would have warned the contractor and then tipped off the Ministry, which is what she decided she would do.

Finishing off the last sip of her delicious beer, Deb got back into her car and drove with a much greater resolve and confidence. She would nail the bastard one way or another.

THIRTY-ONE

I t wasn't difficult finding the address of Wilson
Contractor's as there was a big sign at the entrance to the
property. Deb pulled over and decided to park her car
out on the roadside and walk up the driveway.

There was no sign of life. The house looked like a typical
1970s split-ranch with what would once have been a well
landscaped garden. It now looked decidedly neglected with
empty flowerpots haphazardly stacked in piles by the front
door. Deb knocked on the door and waited. There was no
response. *Oh, shit*, she thought. She had never anticipated the
house being empty.

She looked around the property. There was a large forlorn
looking shed and several other dilapidated buildings and an
old, rusty looking tractor was parked by the side of some metal
drums. There were fields beyond the garden some looking
quite well ploughed whereas others were feet high in weeds.

Deb decided to go for a walk and get the lay of the land.
She knew that if anything had been dumped over forty years
ago, particularly if it had been buried, there would be no

obvious sign, but she felt she needed to see the property for herself.

The field closest to the house had been neatly ploughed and looked ready for planting. Deb pulled out a copy of the marked up topographical map that Hendrich and she had drawn by interpreting from the sampling the likely source of the contamination plume into the river.

They had also made enquiries with local tiling companies and established that the Wilson property had been tiled almost fifty years ago. That meant that anything buried would have to have been put in the ground before the tiling as most field tiles were only about three to four feet into the ground. The manifesto from Vanastra had included a large quantity of electrical appliances plus paints and old conduits and wiring and these may not have been buried, maybe just dumped somewhere on the property.

Deb walked back the way she had come and was about to leave when a van pulled into the driveway. It had its name blazoned on the side, Wilson's Contractor. *Oh hell*, Deb thought, she would have to confront the man after all.

If his body language was anything to go by, she was in for a hard time. Steve Wilson stood squarely with his chest puffed out and a scowl on his face. He was a man probably in his fifties, heavy set, and well weathered.

The contracting business had been in the family for several generations, but now, because of mismanagement on Steve's part, it was failing as a company.

Deb decided to make the first move. "Oh, hi there, I was looking for a Mr. Wilson?"

"I'm Mr. Wilson and what are you doing on my property, I saw you in the field over there."

"Actually, I was looking for you I thought that you might

be in the field." She pointed to the open field she had just come from.

"Umm.... well, how can I help you?" he said reluctantly.

"I think that you might have met my colleague Dr. de Roo, microbiologist? Anyway, we have been working on a research paper together through The University of Western, on Ground Water contamination of the Bayfield River.

From our studies we are pretty sure that a significant source of the groundwater contamination can be traced back to your land. I felt that it was only right to give you notice that we intend to share our findings with the Ministry of the Environment. If we do this, then they will be obliged to investigate thoroughly unless you can help us with locating the actual source of the toxic waste."

"What toxic waste?" Steve snarled, "You people have no right coming here on to private land accusing me of having toxic waste. What proof do you have, tell me, give me one bit of concrete proof that there is toxic waste on my land."

Deb held her ground and waited for him to calm down although she was beginning to feel quite threatened. She pulled out her map and pointed to the circled area marked just up from the river.

"The ground water travels south to the river. We have conducted a longitudinal study on the levels of PCBs in the river water, which I have to say have risen alarmingly over the past two years.

"We are scientists, Mr. Wilson, we deal in facts and figures and the simple fact is we have traced the source of the PCBs back to your land. As to how we have done that, well I could show you the results from hundreds of invertebrates collected from the Bayfield River.

"They all say the same thing, that the toxicity from PCBs

found in the skeletons of the fish are over one thousand times the minimum acceptable levels of PCBs and they are at their highest where the drainage from your land feeds into the river. These are indisputable facts.

"Now, as I said before, you can show me where you dumped the material that we know you took from Vanastra, or I can call in the Ministry and they'll dig everything up until they find the source."

For such a big man, Steve Wilson moved at the speed of lightning. Before Deb could sidestep his attack, he set upon her and with a violent slap of his hand across her face, she was momentarily stunned.

Staggering backwards, Deb tripped on some debris and landed flat on her back, giving Steve time to lift her up and throw her over his shoulder. She found herself being carried like a sack of potatoes over to the shed where he dumped her unceremoniously on top of a pile of seed bags.

Deb attempted to stand up but was roughly pushed down again. Steve grabbed a roll of duct tape and proceeded to bind her hands and feet together and then, finally, her mouth.

"Now you're going to stay here, you bitch, until I can work out what to do with you," he snarled and closed the shed door leaving Deb in semi darkness. There was one small window at the back of the old shed. It was so covered in cobwebs and ingrained with years of dirt that it barely let in any light; however, there was just about sufficient lighting for Deb to make out the doorway and the grass cutter, plus stacks of flowerpots and seed bags.

She desperately sought out some tools: a spade or fork would have been ideal, but there appeared to be no tools anywhere. Maybe she would be able to kick the door open? She was reluctant to make any noise as that would surely bring the monster back and then heaven only knows what he might do to her.

Deb lay on the seed sacks and contemplated her predicament. What would Wilson do with her? How long would it be before she was missed? Tamara, her assistant, would expect her in the office the next day. Also Dave, Sue, and Karen her friends might wonder where she was as they had arranged to meet at the wine bar on Richmond Street that evening. If she didn't show up, they would just put it down to her working late at the university. They might try texting her and no doubt would leave a ton of messages, but that would be the extent of their concern. No, it appeared that she was on her own on this occasion and, somehow, she would just have to outsmart the man herself.

THIRTY-TWO

A fter leaving the Happy Valley Adult Community, John continued his drive towards Vanastra. He drove down Bayfield River Road past the Windmill Lake Eco Park pausing to look at the stunning property and recalled the events that had taken place there the previous year.

The Eco-Park was just gearing up towards another busy season of wakeboarding, paddle boarding, and kayaking. John remembered the lovely owner of the park, such a brave, young woman, not only passionate about her work, but equally passionate about the environment and the dreadful pollution of plastics in the lake. He hoped that she would have another successful season. Trying to establish any business was hard enough itself, but one as unusual as wakeboarding, well, he had to raise his hat to her for her entrepreneurial skills.

At the end of the Bayfield River Road he came to Parr Line, if he turned right that would take him to Varna. He recalled that the Stonehouse Brewery wasn't far away, maybe on his return he would pop in for a pint of their Czech Pilsner. Turning left onto Parr Line, he reached the Bayfield road and turned right heading into Clinton.

Following his GPS, he came down the hill into Clinton through an area of light industry before crossing an old barely used railway line just on the edge of the town and, turning sharply to the right, followed Railway Street to Highway 4. He then turned right again and continued on past the Huron View Nursing Home until he reached the hamlet of Vanastra.

What he found was a semi-derelict old air force base complete with a geodetic dome in a state of disrepair. On closer inspection, he realized that many of the almost identical houses were lived in, and a small community had developed although he couldn't see any shops, but maybe they were close enough to Clinton not to warrant the need for any retail space.

The place had a strange, haunted look about it with a great sense of abandonment, not exactly welcoming. John parked his car on the side of the road by the old geodetic domed building and fished out his notebook. Flicking back several pages he found what he was looking for: Sergeant Flowers' mini lecture on ground water contaminants and PCBs.

He read through his notes carefully. Vanastra was about two kilometres from the Bayfield River. However, what leapt out at him from his notes was the fact that the Royal Canadian Air Force had decommissioned the Radar Training School way back in 1971, removing all the equipment. The contract for that had been awarded to a local contractor. *Could this be Wilson's,* John thought.

He felt the hairs on his neck prickle, a sure sign that he was onto something. Reading through more of his notes John also found that the source of the ground water contaminants entering the river was close to where Parr Line crossed the Bayfield River.

He decided to drive back to Bayfield via Parr Line and see if he could find Wilson's Contractors, possibly somewhere in that location.

THIRTY-THREE

It was another beautiful day. The sky was a clear cobalt blue and the fields green and lush. John felt infused with a sense of well being, he loved living in Canada with its peacefulness and warm, polite people. He had no desire to ever return to the old country, maybe he would end up moving to Huron County from London, but not until Rachel, his daughter, no longer needed his help babysitting. Time would tell when that might be, but for now he was more than happy with the status-quo.

Driving down Parr line John suddenly spotted Dr. Cave's red Toyota parked by the roadside opposite a rather run down 1970s style split-ranch house. Sitting in the driveway was a work van with Wilson Contractor's printed on the side panel. John pulled into the drive and parked his car parallel to the van. He looked around the uncared-for yard. There were upturned flowerpots lying by the front door and what might have been once nice shrubberies, now were overgrown with weeds. The adjacent field had been recently ploughed, *could this be the burial ground for the dumped material?* John thought looking at the recently furrowed field.

Whatever had been buried would have had over forty years of decomposition and leaching into the ground water. Could the owner of the property be challenged outright, or should he leave all of that to the authorities? He was still not convinced that any of the groundwater issues had a single thing to do with the murder.

John was jerked out of his reveries by the front door being suddenly flung open, a rough looking man in his early fifties appeared. He walked over to John, crossing his arms over his chest, and stood there with a scowl on his face.

"What can I do for you?" he said gruffly.

"I noticed my friend's car parked out on the roadside. Is she inside as I would like to have a word with her?"

"No, there is no one else here and I would like you to leave my property right now. You're trespassing."

"Hold your horses, mate." John said, "I just wanted to have a word with my friend, but if you say that she's not here, then where is she? Her car is parked over there." John pointed out to the road.

"Well, as I said, there is no one here. She must have taken herself for a walk. Now clear off my land before I set my dog on you."

John turned to leave, but just as he was about to get into his car, he heard a loud thud coming from an old shed to the side of the house. He paused and then started to walk towards the shed. He had just reached the building when he felt a great bang on his head. His world started to spin, and he found himself falling into oblivion.

Deb had been kicking on the shed door as hard as she could until her legs felt as if they would give out on her. She suddenly sensed someone approaching and was hit by a waft of fresh air as the door to the shed was thrown open and heard something being dragged inside. The next sound she heard was the sound of duct tape being wound around someone or something. Then the fresh air was once again cut off as the door to the shed was closed. What or who had been dumped in with her?

THIRTY-FOUR

Rose and Susan got back to the village shortly after two that afternoon. Neither of them felt that they had achieved much, and both felt a trifle depressed and down in spirits. As Susan pulled into Rose's driveway she said, "I think that tomorrow we should drive back out to the scene of the crime. What's really bugging me is where the heck is Hendrich's cell phone? The USRU thoroughly searched the riverbed and I'm sure that they would have found it if it were there in the water. I think that it might be on the riverbank somewhere and Rose we're going to find it."

"If you say so, Susan, we will search like dogs tomorrow, but right now I have two beasts desperately needing a walk and you have one fluff ball probably waiting for you to come and play. What time should we meet in the morning?"

"Let's get an early start, say meet at nine, and then afterwards we can drive down Parr Line and see if we can locate where the contaminated groundwater source begins. Okay, see you tomorrow."

Rose waved to Susan as she zoomed off in her flashy Porsche. She opened the front door to the sound of two barking dogs. They were definitely ready for a walk.

Susan got back inside her condo to find mayhem. Her plant pot containing a beautiful white orchid had been knocked over leaving a trail of dirt all over the floor. The hall rug was all puckered up and Fluffy's water and food bowls turned upside down. Peeping out from behind a scatter cushion the little kitten meowed.

"Oh Fluffy, what on earth have you been up to?"

Susan could not be angry as the little kitten had obviously become bored and had run amok in the living room. A quick tidy up and all would be restored back to normal. She would be meeting John later that evening, but before she did Susan wanted to take stock of what Rose and she had learned, as she was not convinced that the ground water study had anything to do with the murder.

Susan just wanted to know what John and his team had uncovered and hoped that over some drinks she might get some useful information about the status of the case. Then, if she could get a hold of the facts of the case, they wouldn't be chasing false leads. But for now, though, Fluffy needed to be played with and a nice, long soak in the hot tub would also go down a treat.

Rose did her best thinking either when she was baking or going for a walk. She gathered up the dogs, put them on their leashes and proceeded to walk down Bayfield Terrace towards the lake. She would let the dogs off their leashes when she got to the beach and let them go for a swim while she sat on the sand and did some serious thinking.

It did appear to Rose that there were three strands to the

murder investigation and somehow all three had got tangled up together. The first strand was the pharmaceutical company and their refusal to acknowledge Hendrich's paper on the use of sodium chlorite as a cure for pathogenic diseases.

She had Googled cures for pathogens and to her surprise had found other similar findings that supported Dr. de Roo's discovery. But would the pharmaceutical company go as far as to silence the doctor in his attempts to promote an easy cure? Rose thought that would be far too extreme an action, but wondered about sodium chlorite, she knew that it was commonly used to purify water and to sterilize, but to be used as a medicine she had never heard of this before, although it did make sense to her. If one wanted to purify drinking water which contained pathogens one would use this and a few other similar sterilizing chemicals like sodium chlorite. If the body already had been infected with pathogens, it would be perfectly logical to use the same chemicals to prevent infection, at least that was what made sense to Rose.

The second confusing strand was the academic research that both doctors had collaborated on together, groundwater contamination and the toxic fall out of PCBs, could that be the motive for murder? Thinking about the academic side of the case, Rose wondered how Doctor Cave was respected in the microbiology department at the University of Western? Beyond doubt Doctor de Roo had been held in the high esteem worldwide, but she wasn't so sure about Doctor Cave.

Finally, the third strand was the oldest and most plausible and that was the possibility of the murder being a crime of passion? The love angle of possible rejection and hurt or otherwise, could Dr. Cave have been in love with Dr. de Roo and if so, what could have provoked her to murder?

Thinking about the different strands to the case gave Rose no real clarity, but it had enabled her to separate the possible motives for murder. She had an inkling that the love angle might be the most promising one to pursue.

THIRTY-FIVE

Susan waited at the bar of The Little Inn for John to arrive. She had dressed carefully wearing a light pair of cream linen pants and a coral silk tunic top, her auburn hair glowed with health and was worn to her shoulders, and she sported coral earrings and a matching pendant.

After waiting an hour of for him to arrive while nursing a gin and tonic, and after endlessly checking the time, and sending several text messages, Susan gave up and, feeling thoroughly disappointed, drove back home. She had been so looking forward to meeting up with John again and to picking his brain about the case.

Rose, meanwhile, had been telling Tom about Anne and Allan's separation. Tom's reaction to the news had somewhat irritated her as, instead of feeling sorry for his daughter, he had taken Allan's side saying, "Surely, love, she can forgive him. He must have been so bored staying at home being a house-father, no wonder he craved a bit of excitement."

Rose had been really angry with him, but before she could

say anything more the phone rang. It was Jessica from Montreal.

"Mom, have you heard about Anne and Allan? I don't blame her for giving him his marching orders, what a slime ball."

Rose had just finished her conversation with Jessica when the phone rang again. This time it was Paul from London. "Mom, I just heard that Anne and Allan are splitting up. Is it true? I really like Allan, he's a stellar guy. Surely, they'll make up. What about the kids?"

Paul and his wife Atsuko had themselves split up and for almost two years they had lived apart until after Atsuko's father died and Paul had flown out to the funeral. They had then reconciled and now had a beautiful baby boy, Yuki.

Rose felt sad and depressed herself but reflected on how quickly bad news travelled. She was aware that their kids texted each other all the time, something that Tom and she never did, but that was the most common and cheapest way to communicate, also, the most instant.

Thinking about this made Rose wonder about Hendrich and his means of communication. If he truly was an absent-minded professor and was in a relationship with Doctor Cave, even he, the reclusive scientist, would most certainly have been forced to communicate by phone, if nothing else other than to please his partner.

We have to find that phone, she thought as there would most certainly be a record of their messages if they were indeed in a relationship, and possibly there within, a motive for murder.

Susan and she would have to go back out to the scene of the crime and really search in the shrubs and bushes of the surrounding area. The phone, Rose was convinced, could hold the key to solving the murder.

THIRTY-SIX

J ohn opened his eyes and blinked, he was in the shed of that he was sure, and there was someone else in the dusty space with him. His arms were tied behind his back with duct tape, and his ankles were also bound.

Duct tape had also been bound around his mouth which made it impossible for him to talk. He managed to sit up and could make out the outline of Deb Cave wedged against the other side of the shed and what looked like a grass mower between them.

It was also pitch-black inside because the small glass window was so ingrained with dirt that it blocked out the light. John hadn't a clue how long he had lain there, all he knew was that his head was throbbing like a drum and his mouth felt as dry as sandpaper.

He tried to pull his hands apart, but they were taped palm to palm and impossible to move even his fingers, his ankles were also strapped tightly, but he was able to wriggle his feet. He was acutely aware of Deb trying to get his attention with her eyes. She had managed to kick off her shoes and was using her toes to pick up what looked like a nail from the dirty floor. She shuffled on her bottom over to John and placed the nail wedged between her toes, carefully into his hands. Right, they were finally in business.

Half an hour later, John had just succeeded in freeing his wrists of the duct tape when the shed door suddenly swung open. Steve Wilson stood there and immediately noticed John's free hand.

"Oh no you don't, just as well I came in when I did, now I'm going to have to re-tape your wrists and I want to collect your cell phones and car keys. You see, I'm not going to leave anything to chance. I'm not as ignorant as you hoped. I know, and you know, that anyone can be tracked by their GPS on their phones. I need both your keys so that I can move your cars, particularly your bright red car it's like a bloody siren."

He proceeded to remove Deb's phone and keys from her pocket then went to retrieve John's when suddenly John let out a mighty kick aimed at Steve's groin. He yelled out in pain and kicked John back snarling, "If you ever do that again I'll have to get my hunting rifle. Now, I'm going to be putting you in the back of my van, you can either come quietly or I can hit you over your head again and send you back to oblivion. Which is it to be then? I recommend compliancy. Okay, I'll take the lady first, but I'm going to blind fold you both so that you're going to have to shuffle over to the van holding my arm. Right, are you ready?"

Deb was hauled up to her feet and a dirty smelling bandana was tied around her head covering up her eyes. She was led unceremoniously to the back of his van and tossed in so that she was lying on her back. He did the same with John, although pushing him into the van proved somewhat more difficult because of his size and bulk.

Finally, both Deb and John lay side by side on the floor of the van and they were driven over what felt like rutted land, certainly not a paved road. Only a few minutes of driving before the van pulled up and the doors were flung open.

John had managed to loosen his blindfold and could make out the shape of an old timber building. They were in the middle of a forest made up mostly of sugar maples, and behind what was now clearly a sugar shack was a small mountain of piled up junk ranging from old fridges to office equipment to fans, all piled on top of each other in one large, rusty dump.

Ironically, this was most likely the source of the contaminated groundwater, but neither of them was aware of their close proximity to the toxic waste.

The sugar shack wasn't in such a bad shape as the old shed. In fact, Steve Wilson had made maple syrup every year and kept the utensils and the equipment in the shed in good working order. The middle of the shack was taken up with the condenser and a great big trough which took up most of the limited space. John and Deb were pushed into the tight area without a single word from Steve. They could hear him panting with excursion and were relieved when he finally drove off leaving them to contemplate their situation.

John was the first to rub his face up against the wall of the shack and free the bandana from his head. Being able to see clearly again gave him a huge surge of hope. Deb followed soon after repeating his rubbing action to remove her blindfold. The only light in the sugar shack was from what little managed to filter through the rough-hewn planks of the structure.

It was sufficient, though, for John and Deb to make out the

maple syrup equipment and the outline of the doorway. Their eyes eagerly sought out something that could be used to cut through the duct tape, but there was nothing obvious at hand. Both of them feeling somewhat deflated, slumped back down onto the dirt floor and reviewed their situation.

THIRTY-SEVEN

Rose woke up with a start, she picked up her phone, turned it on and checked the date. "Oh," she groaned, "Oh my, oh my," and she poked Tom in his ribs to wake him up. "Tom, it's Abby's birthday, we forgot. Oh my gosh, we've never forgotten any of our grandkid's birthdays. Oh, dear, oh dear. I'm such a bad grandma."

Tom looked at her with bleary eyes, half asleep and not really comprehending her distress.

"Eh, love, umm...go back to sleep."

"Oh, but Tom, I feel so bad. I've never, ever, forgotten one of our children's birthdays, let alone one of our grandchildren."

"There's nothing you can do about it at six in the morning, love. Look, we'll send one of those e-cards and then go on Amazon and order something, if you say that her present is in the mail then you can blame it on Canada post."

"Oh, well, I suppose you're right, Tom. I'll phone Abby later and wish her a happy birthday. Right, I'll go and make us a pot of tea."

Tom had closed his eyes again and fallen back to sleep. By the time Rose came back to the bedroom with two steaming mugs of tea, he was well and truly snoring away and back into la-la land.

Rose got out her notebook and started to make a list of all the loose ends that Susan and she had to tie up to try and make some sense of Hendrich de Roo's murder.

SUSAN HAD ALSO WOKEN up early with a sense of urgency she could not explain. Being stood up by John Hargreaves with no explanation had left her feeling strangely uneasy. She knew that he was not the kind of man that would cancel a date without having a good reason for doing so and now she wondered if he had been involved in an accident or something else more sinister.

After breakfast, and before her run, she would try phoning him again. She got out of bed and padded down to the kitchen where she found Fluffy playing with a cloth mouse stuffed with catnip that Susan had bought from the pet store in Goderich.

Putting the kettle on, Susan grabbed her phone and trolled through her emails. There was one from her husband, Tone. She opened it nervously, scanning the short text Susan let out an exasperated cry. For one small moment she had thought that he might be writing to let her know that he was coming home, but no, Tone was begging her for more money that he owed for his gambling debts. *So absolutely nothing had changed,* Susan thought, *Tone hadn't even tried.*

She had stopped sending him money months ago and when she hadn't heard from him, she had foolishly hoped that he had stopped gambling. As to the drugs, well she had ratio-nalized that if he didn't have any money then he wouldn't be able to buy the drugs he so craved. How could she have been so naïve? Addicts were very resourceful when it came down to finding ways to feed their habit. This felt like the last straw; she was ready now to file for divorce and be done with it.

Having consumed two cups of coffee and one yogurt, Susan put on her running shoes and started to jog down towards the marina. Not all the boats had been put in the water yet, but there were sufficient to make a colourful array. She saw Rose and Tom's boat, *Tranquillity*, moored close to the club house. Running down past the main car park Susan had an excellent view of the progress of the new bridge construction. It was rising up out of the water like some majestic monolith.

The abutments both sides of the river, which would support the whole structure, were in place. The spanning beams would be constructed next and finally the metal beams would be laid to form the support for the road. The overall finished structure would curve and span gracefully across, connecting the two abutments. It would be a fine bridge when completed.

From her vantage point, Susan could also see the Bayfield River Flats and where the body of Hendrich de Roo had been found. It seemed such a waste of a genius, a man dedicated to science who had kept himself to himself just wanting to work on his precious research. She knew that her friend Rose had promised his mother that she would do everything she could to find out who had murdered her son. Whether it was Rose and she who succeeded or DCI Hargreaves and his team, one thing was for certain, justice would be served one way or another.

Susan completed her run and checked her watch. It was eight-thirty, time for a quick shower and then another call to see if she could get a hold of John before she met up with Rose at nine.

THIRTY-EIGHT

The team all sat around the large conference table down in the basement of the town hall waiting for their boss; he had never been this late before and there was an unspoken ripple of concern in the air.

Finally Constable Holly said, "Well, I'm going to phone him." Which she proceeded to do only to find that the call went straight to voicemail. "I'll try texting him then," but still no response. "Okay, does anyone have any idea where he could be?"

Sergeant Flowers said that he would call The Little Inn as maybe he could be ill and still in bed.

The Little Inn however said that as far as they knew he was not in the hotel, and that he had not shown up for breakfast.

"Right, who else might know where he's got to?"

"He's friendly with the Blair's." Constable Brown chipped in, "Should I call them?"

Sergeant Flowers nodded his head and the Constable put in the call. Tom answered.

"Tom speaking."

"Tom, we're trying to get in touch with DCI Hargreaves, have you seen or heard from him recently?"

Tom said that he had seen him the previous afternoon in The Albion but then the whole team had been there with him. He called over to Rose.

"Rose, love, have you or Susan seen John Hargreaves recently?"

Rose answered, "Susan was meeting him for a drink last night. That's about all I know."

Tom relayed this to Constable Brown who put his phone down and said, "Look, guys, he might have had a date with Susan Parker and umm... well, gone back to her place and umm... maybe overslept or something?"

Sergeant Flowers said, "But he would have still answered his phone, wouldn't he? Look let's give it another half an hour and then we'll review the situation. I'll go and get us all some coffee from Shop Bike while we wait, okay?"

THIRTY-NINE

R
ose turned up at Susan's condo bang on 9:00 a.m., she found Susan playing with Fluffy, but also looking a bit worried.

"Hi, there friend, what's up?"

"I'm just a bit concerned, Rose, as John and I were supposed to have had a drink together last night, but he never showed up and I haven't been able to reach him by phone."

"That's strange, Constable Brown just phoned Tom to ask if he had seen or heard from John recently. Wow, I wonder what's going on."

Rose had an involuntary flash shoot through her mind of John and her sister sleeping in after a night of passionate sex, she quickly erased the image in her head and said, "I'll phone Kate and see if she's seen or heard from him."

Kate answered the phone at the first ring.

"Oh, hi Rose, what's up?"

"Kate, have you heard from John recently? We're trying to reach him."

"Only yesterday at The Albion, he was there with his team

and Tom, Gary, and Peter. He invited me out to join him for dinner tonight at The Little Inn."

Another prickle of jealousy coursed through Rose, but she stamped on it and said her goodbyes to Kate and turned to Susan.

"It appears that John has disappeared, look, let's go out to the scene of the crime and search for that cell phone. I'm sure that his team will track him down and I'm equally sure that there will be some simple explanation, but it's still a bit worrying."

Susan and Rose headed out and arrived at The Happy Valley Adult Community Trailer Park, just as Wilson's Contractors panel van roared off in the opposite direction.

"Blimey, he's in a might hurry," Rose said as she pulled over to let the van pass. "Do you think that by some remote chance Wilson is the contractor used by the Ministry to remove all the electrical items from the old Radar School at Vanastra? We should make some enquiries about them."

"Honestly, Rose, are you still harping on about that toxic waste? You do realize that it is over forty years since anything was dumped and there is a strong possibility that the contractor, whoever he might be, could easily no longer be in business."

As they parked the car Rose noticed Helen in her front garden planting out some small succulent plants. She waved to her as they walked towards the embankment.

"That Helen would probably know more about the local contractors than anyone else, we'll have a word with her before we leave."

Down by the river the yellow police tape flickered in the breeze, but it did serve a purpose by helping Rose and Susan focus on the area of search for the phone.

"So, if the phone was not flung into the river where could it possibly have been thrown?" Rose asked. "Look, I'm going to mimic throwing it and I want you, Susan to watch where my arm direction takes you."

"Better still, Rose, throw this rock and see where it lands."

Rose grabbed the small rock and threw it like she was throwing a baseball. They watched where it landed and walked over through the undergrowth to find it. Scouring the surrounding area, they did not find the phone. They repeated the throwing action in different directions four times, still to no avail.

Finally, when they were about to give up, Susan took the rock and slammed it into the bushes closest to Hendrich's house. Rose tramped over and began to search again muttering that it was like trying to find a needle in a haystack.

She bent over and pulled back a clump of weeds and there lo behold, lying in the dirt, was the cellphone.

"Bingo, I've found it." she called out and handed it over to Susan, "what now?"

As they would not be able to open up the phone to read the text messages without Hendrich's password, they would have to hand the phone over to the investigating team who had professional IT people. They would be able to unlock the phone in minutes and, as it would be out of their hands then, they would probably never get to know the contents of the phone. Susan and Rose contemplated this as they walked back up the embankment.

Arriving back at the car Helen waved her hand at them in a beckoning motion and invited them over to enjoy a glass of iced tea with Bill and her.

The excitement of finding the phone had now been

replaced with indecision. Rose walked towards Helen and Bill's trailer and Susan followed behind deep in thought.

"We'd love some iced tea." she said. Helen pulled up a couple of garden chairs and they sat under a brightly coloured umbrella and sipped the delicious beverage.

"You detectives don't give up, do you? That handsome one, you know the dark-skinned detective, he was here again yesterday afternoon asking more questions. Are you getting any closer to finding the murderer?"

Susan told Helen about finding the phone and how they were hopeful that it might hold the key to some unanswered questions.

"The only trouble is we don't know the password to open it up."

Bill, who had been sitting listening to the conversation, perked up at the mention of passwords.

"Hey, give that phone to me, I bet you that I'll be able to crack open the code in a few minutes." He tapped his head, "It's my brain you know, it's wired up differently than most; I can see patterns and sequences in everything, can't I love?"

Helen beamed with pride at her husband. "Yes, our Bill is a genius with technology. He built his own radio tower years before cellphones had been invented. Yes, if anyone can unlock this phone, it's our Bill."

Rose and Susan exchanged a hopeful glance, suddenly finding the phone felt like a major break-through in the case, they waited with baited-breath while Bill tinkered with the phone.

Ten minutes later he let out a triumph, "Here you are, it's unlocked. I tried out various numerical sequences; his was based on multiples of three, 3927, just remember that will you both."

Rose and Susan thanked him effusively. Taking the phone from Bill and finishing up their iced tea they headed back to the car.

"Come on, Susan, open it up. Let's see what text messages he has." Rose said with a note of impatience to her voice.

They spent the following five minutes scrolling through messages primarily from Deb Cave to Hendrich. It was pretty obvious from the content that Deb and Hendrich were lovers, but a love that had suddenly turned sour.

The last day of messages, the day before Hendrich had been murdered, Deb's texting had turned nasty. She accused him of not supporting her application for tenureship at the university, blamed him for not helping her enough with the paper she was writing, accused him of receiving all the accolade for the research work that she had primarily conducted herself, and finally she threatened to sue him for plagiarism.

"Wow, a woman scorned, she definitely sounds as if she could be our murderer." Rose said, but she noticed Susan still looking sceptical.

"It's all still just circumstantial evidence, Rose, no solid proof, and look, I've just come across a text message from Barry Brown of Santé Industries, he had arranged a meeting with our doctor and guess when the meeting was scheduled?"

"Don't tell me, the day Hendrich was murdered? Oh Susan, that really puts the cat amongst the pigeons, doesn't it? Anyway, there is nothing we can do about it right now so let's continue to Parr Line and see if we can find our contractor. Oh, shoot, we were going to ask Helen and Bill about Wilsons Contractor, weren't we?"

"Don't worry, Rose, I'm on to it, I'll just Google Wilson Contractors and see what comes up."

Rose drove while Susan used her smart phone. Soon she

looked up from the screen and said, "Good old Google, it looks like Wilsons Contractors have been in business now for fifty years. Used to be called Wilson Contractor and Son, but after his father died in 1995 his son, Steve, took over the business and changed the name. It seems that they don't actually do any construction work anymore, mostly just maintenance work. Didn't Helen call him their go to guy?"

"Yes, you're right, she did. Does it give an address?"

"Yes, it's on Parr Line; Rose, we're onto something here, this Wilsons Contractor might be the same contractor that won the contract to move all the electrical stuff from the radar school.

"According to Doctor Cave's assistant, the source of the contamination is around Parr Line, it's just too much of a coincidence that the groundwater source originated from the same area as the contractor's property. Do you think that maybe DCI Hargreaves and Doctor Cave also found out the address and that's where they both are right now? We definitely need to investigate this property,"

Rose agreed. They were already heading in the direction of Parr Line; it would do no harm checking out the address of the contractor.

FORTY

few minutes later Rose, who had been pondering the situation said, "Do you think Doctor Cave found the contractor? Wasn't she on a mission to confront him? You know, Susan, I don't like the sound of this. By the tone of her texting, Doctor Cave is pretty pushy; she might just have pushed too far with the contractor."

They drove the rest of the way in silence and soon they reached the address Susan had found on Google Search. They pulled up on the side of the road outside the property and looked down the driveway, there was no sign of life or indeed of any cars.

"I think that we should go and walk around the property. I'm pretty certain there's no one around, but if we bump into anyone then we can just say that we are looking for DCI Hargreaves."

Soon Susan and Rose were walking down the driveway taking in the rundown house and out-buildings. Rose pointed to behind the shed where she could see the nose of a car poking out.

"Susan, that looks like John's car. Let's go and see."

Sure enough, DCI Hargreaves car was parked alongside Deb Cave's red Toyota. Both cars were hidden out of view from the road. If they hadn't have got out of their car and walked around, they would have missed seeing the concealed vehicles.

"Okay, if their cars are here then, where are they?" Rose said feeling more and more apprehensive.

"I've got a bad feeling about this." Susan said, "I think that I'll call Sergeant Flowers and let the team know that we've found the cars."

Susan tapped in Sergeant Flowers number and was relieved when he answered almost straight away.

"Sergeant, Rose Blair and I are out on Parr Line, and we've found DCI Hargreaves and Doctor Cave's vehicles. There is no sign of either of them or for that matter, the owner of the property."

"Thank you, umm...Susan, we've been looking for DCI Hargreaves all morning. Text me the address and I'll send the team out there immediately. Do you think that our man is dangerous?"

"I honestly don't know, but he's a farmer so he probably owns a gun. My guess is that he has them holed up somewhere, Rose and I will snoop around and see what we can find out while we wait for you."

"Just be careful, we'll be there in about ten minutes, in the meantime, don't do anything rash."

Susan texted the address, put away her phone and beckoned to Rose to follow. The shed looked like the obvious place to hide someone.

When they got to the building it was obvious that someone had been there, and not too long ago either. There were scuff marks on the floor and what looked like a long rusty nail. The giveaway was a pair of socks which had been kicked off and now lay screwed up on the floor.

Susan picked them up and examined the label. They were Calvin Klein silk ladies' socks in a small foot size.

"I could see Dr. Cave wearing these, couldn't you, Susan?"

"Well, as we've never met the woman I don't know, but sure, she must be in her late twenties or early thirties I would imagine and probably quite good looking, but yes, I reckon they could be her socks; they're certainly not John's. Okay, so for the sake of an argument let's assume that she was shut in this shed, where would she then be taken? What does our man intend to do with her?"

"Maybe he has them locked in the house. I think I'm going to walk around the property and try to look into the windows, what do you think, Susan?"

"I think that we should get the hell out of here and wait for the team to get here.
"

They both walked back to their car and once inside Rose began to talk in a slightly manic way.

"I'm feeling more than a little confused right now, Susan. What on earth has any of this got to do with the murder? I was thinking that the prime suspect was Doctor Cave, but now I don't know. Could it be the contractor?"

"I don't honestly know, Rose, but one thing is for certain, we have to find DCI Hargreaves and the doctor and soon."

FORTY-ONE

John and Deb had spent an uncomfortable night sitting on the cold dirt floor of the sugar shack with their backs pressed against the wall. They were still searching for something to use to cut through the duct tape tied around their wrists. John was trying to break the tape by pushing his hands against the edge of the galvanized bucket he had found on the floor. Deb was also trying to break the tape around her wrists by rubbing her wrists over the condenser. They were both exhausted and thirsty as hell.

John knew that his team would be out searching for him and that Sergeant Flowers would have pulled out all stops to find them assuming they had worked out where they actually were. He only hoped that they wouldn't be too long as heaven only knew what Steve Wilson planned to do with them when he returned to the sugar shack. He was like a time bomb just waiting to explode.

Looking around the gloomy interior of the sugar shack, John realized that in their endeavours to find something to use to break through the duct tape, neither Deb nor he had really studied the planked walls of the shack. Surely utensils like ladles would be hung from somewhere accessible like a wall. John shuffled over to the wall and started to scan the surface using what little light there was to see what he was doing.

Nothing appeared to be hanging on any of the four walls, but just as he was about to give up on finding a nail in the wall, he noticed a large knot hole in one of the planks of wood. It was at a perfect height for him to raise his wrists and begin to rub them against the jagged edge of the knot. He felt the skin of his hands roughen like sandpaper as he pulled his wrists up and down over the woody knot. Blood speckled the wall and John bit his lips with pain as splinters of wood pushed their way into his skin, but then he was free. He pulled his hands apart, stretched his numb fingers and let out a triumph shout of joy.

"Deb, I'm free. Just hold on and give me a few minutes to release my ankles and I'll come and free your hands for you."

John eventually found the end of the duct tape wrapped around his ankles and finally managed to unwind and free his feet. Being able to walk again greatly improved his spirits and soon Deb and he were gleefully rubbing their wrists and ankles and getting ready to escape the sugar-shack.

"We need to make haste and go before he comes back; heaven knows what he has planned for us."

Fortunately, the door to the sugar-shack was not locked. Looking at the building from the outside John thought it looked like a puff of wind could easily blow it over as it was old and decrepit. He took stock of the surrounding woods and then pointed to what looked like a tall building nestled behind the trees. He beckoned to Deb to follow him keeping their voices down to a minimum. Soon they were in a clearing and what he had mistaken for a building was in fact a huge dump of rusty electrical items: fans, typewriters, old stoves, fridges, washing machines, photocopiers, metal chairs, desks, and even an old tractor.

"Phew, well I guess we've found where Wilsons Contractors dumped their cache from Vanastra. You probably wouldn't understand the importance of this find, John, but this is the source of the contaminated river water. Over the past forty years the chemicals from these electrical machines have leeched into the groundwater and drained into the Bayfield River. Our PCB readings were over ten times the normal, which believe me, John, is very scary."

"Did you or Doctor de Roo contact the authorities about these readings?" John asked Deb.

"Not yet. You do have to understand that research work is not instant and in order to substantiate your results you have to study the levels of contamination over a period of time. Hendrich and I were dissecting the mud feeders, looking at the abnormalities in their skeletons, and measuring the toxin in their bodies. Our results were ready to be published when Hendrich was murdered."

"So, having discovered this dump what will you do now?"

"The Ministry of the Environment will be called in and Wilson's could be fined a huge amount, could be up to a million dollars. The clean-up will take years, but it will have to be done. You know that they closed the Holmesville dump because it was full and it's possible that there could be the same thing happening there. They only take recycling now and all other items like electrical and paints must be dealt with separately. It is a massive problem just exactly what to do with all the potentially toxic waste material that consumers the world over disregard so flippantly."

John was very quiet as he thought about the consequences of groundwater contamination.

"But surely only people with drinking water wells could be affected by this contamination? Like in Walkerton with its e-coli outbreak?"

"Yes, Provincial Water Quality Regulations require that municipalities and water operators of municipal water systems screen very carefully for PCBs and other toxins and pathogens. Hendrich was more interested in pathogenicity in water, the carriers of diseases like Lyme, Bilharzia, West Nile, Malaria and, of course, the plague. He actually was up there on the world stage of leaders in the fields of microbiology and pathogenesis."

"I know, I spent some time reading through some of his research papers which, of course, were mostly way above my head, but I did get the general gist of what he was about and quite honestly it quite scared the heebie-jeebies out of me. Anyway, enough of our talking, we need to get ourselves out of here before our not so friendly contractor finds us missing from the sugar-shack."

"Yes, I know, but how will I ever find this place again? We seem to be in the middle of a forest. How far do you think we travelled from the shed to this shack?"

"Not very far, certainly no more than a kilometre or two, but we were not on a paved road. I reckon he drove us down a rutted farm track. Did you get the lay of the land before he attacked you?"

"Yes, I walked into a field to one side of his property and there was a track of sorts around the edge of the field with trees at one end. If we go back to the sugar-shack and look for a path big enough to take a vehicle then we could follow that and I'm sure it would lead us back to the field. Parr Line runs to the West of the field."

The two of them traipsed back to the shack and found a beaten trail just wide enough to take the van. They followed this track out of the woods until, just as Deb had predicted, they found themselves at the edge of a ploughed field. They would be totally exposed once they left the safety of the tree's; John wondered how visible they would be from the house. Hopefully, Steve Wilson would be out and about working, but they would have to edge their way around stealthily towards the road. There would be absolutely no point in even trying to retrieve their vehicles as he had taken their keys and phones. They would have to make it to Parr Line and rely on being picked up by someone and driven back to Bayfield.

FORTY-TWO

Rose and Susan sat in the car wondering how long it would be before Sergeant Flowers and his team arrived. They had said ten minutes, but that time had already passed.

"I think that we should go. They have the address on Parr Line so there is no real need for us to be here." Susan said.

They were about to pull away when Wilson's panel van turned into the drive. Steve parked his van and jumped out. He marched over to where Susan and Rose were parked and grabbed open the door.

"I'm sick and tired of you lot pestering me, what do you want now?"

Rose, who felt decidedly alarmed when her door had been yanked open, said calmly, "Get your filthy hands off my car."

Susan interrupted, "We're looking for DCI Hargreaves and Doctor Cave and noticed their cars parked behind your shed. Can you enlighten us?"

Steve Wilson looked as if he was going to throw a fit. He slammed the door shut and stomped back to his house, disappearing inside, but returning minutes later with a hunting rifle. He stood at the end of the driveway and pointed it at Rose's Volvo.

"Get going before I shoot." he shouted.

Rose did not hesitate; she drove off so fast that she spun the wheels throwing up gravel like a flurry of snow in the winter.

Just as they reached Bayfield River Road, they saw Sergeant Flowers and his team pull up to the stop sign at the junction. Rose flashed her lights to get their attention, they pulled up alongside the Volvo and wound down their windows.

"The man has a gun and he's on the war path. Be very careful how you approach him." Susan said urgently, "You might have to call in the SWAT team."

It would take time to assemble the SWAT crew which were based in London and Sergeant Flowers wasn't sure what to do. Leadership had never been his strength as he had always relied on his boss. He looked to Susan Parker pleadingly, Susan recognized the panic and indecision in his eyes.

"Sergeant, there are four of you plus, Rose and I, we should be able to overpower one man."

"But he has a gun, and we have no weapons." Sergeant Flowers replied nervously.

"Well maybe we have the element of surprise." Constable Holly chirped in. "If we approach his property from the back and sides, we could have him surrounded."

Sergeant Flowers still looked uncertain. Susan spoke with authority.

"Sensibly put, Constable Ryan, now I think you're onto something. Rose and I walked around the immediate property and there appears to be open fields each side and woods beyond. If we leave our cars down the road and far enough away from his house not to be seen, we can go in by foot. When we have encircled the property one of us can distract the man while the rest of the team move in and overtake him. Any questions?"

Constable Brown also looked nervous. "What about the rifle? What's going to stop him from shooting the person in front?"

"Training, officer, training." Susan said a trifle impatiently, "You've all been trained for combat, now is the time to put that training into action, okay, who wants to be the decoy?"

They all looked at each other and then Constable Ryan said, "I'll do it, you guys can tackle him better than me."

"Okay, then that's settled, let's do it." Susan said. "Just follow Rose and me and we'll find a place to park and then we'll all go in by foot."

FORTY-THREE

R ose turned her Volvo around and drove back down Parr Line, knowing the location of the property really helped, they were able to find a spot to park in a natural lay-by in the bend of the road far enough away to be hidden from view. The four team members got out and Rose and Susan joined them.

"These fields all join up and I'm sure are all part of Wilson's property. If we keep to the perimeter and go in pairs stealthily, we should be able to get behind and both sides of the property. Constable Ryan you can hold back until we're all in place and then you should approach the property front on. Right, off we go and remember that it's imperative that we approach in stealth, he must not be aware of our approach."

"Umm... what do you want me to do?" Rose asked tentatively. Susan appeared to have taken control of the situation and she suddenly felt somewhat superfluous to the operation.

"Rose, you need to stay in the car, but drive up to the property, not close enough for him to see you though. The team will need rides back to their car after the take-down."

Take down, Rose thought, it sounded like something out of a Western movie. Susan seemed to be in her element and Rose thought that she herself would just go along with it all and stay out of the way of any action. She conceded that she was a liability as a civilian, not an asset, as she had no tactical training.

They reached the field at the edge of the property and Sergeant Flowers and Constable Elliot veered off to the right to approach the house from the other side. Constable Ryan and Constable Brown continued to walk to the property entrance with Susan following at a distance.

"Cover me from here. "Constable Ryan said as she stepped forward and walked towards the house.

As expected, Steve Wilson appeared, rifle in his hands and pointed it at Holly.

"I don't believe it, not another trespassing busybody. I suppose you're with the police too. Now get off my property before I have to shoot."

"I would advice you, sir, to lay down your weapon." Holly said boldly.

"Or what?" snarled Steve.

"You are surrounded by Police. Just do the sensible thing and surrender now before you get hurt."

It just so happened that DCI Hargreaves and Doctor Deb Cave appeared at the edge of the field stopping Steve right in his tracks.

"What the hell are you two doing here?" With that he fired his rifle.

Holly, who had been standing in front of Steve, suddenly felt her shoulder spin and her whole-body whirl around with the impact of the bullet as it seared through her shoulder. Just as she was about to fall, Susan ran out and caught her and then all hell let loose. John came charging out of the field like a rabid bull, he threw his large body headfirst into Steve like a battering ram, knocking the rifle out of his hands and falling to the ground. Sergeant Flowers and Constable Elliot leapt on top of them and for a few minutes it looked like a Rugby scrum.

Steve was finally dragged off the ground with his arm pulled back behind him. Susan, in the meantime, had called for an ambulance and Rose, having heard the shot, had driven her car up to the drive and witnessed all four men dragging Steve Wilson up off the ground. She rolled down her window and said,

"I'll take you back to your car and you can bring him in. I'll come back for Susan, and we'll wait for the paramedics to get here."

Deb came up to the men and reminded John that Steve Wilson had their car keys and cell phones. He had stuffed them in the glove box of his van.

"Sergeant, you go with Constables Brown and Elliot and take this slime ball straight to the OPP station on Highway 21. I'll go with Constable Ryan to the hospital and follow the ambulance in my car. Rose and Susan, thank you so much but you need to go home now and Deb, you too. You'll want to get back to London and rest up. I'll be in touch and get a statement from you another day."

FORTY-FOUR

The ambulance siren could be heard getting louder and louder. Susan, who had been kneeling by Constable Ryan's side putting pressure on the wound whilst talking gently to her, looked up and breathed a sigh of relief.

"Thank God they're here. You'll be in good hands now, Holly. You will be alright."

The paramedics jumped out and within minutes they had Holly strapped onto a gurney and into the ambulance.

Susan watched as Sergeant Flowers, Constables Brown, and Elliot pushed Steve Wilson roughly into Rose's Volvo and then Rose drove the short distance to the team's car, about the same time as the ambulance, but in the opposite direction. She dropped the officers and Steve Wilson off at their car and then returned for Susan. John was about to leave to get his car along with Deb, so that he could follow the ambulance, when Susan remembered about finding the cellphone at Dr. de Roo's cottage.

"Oh John, in all the commotion we forgot to let you know

that Rose and I found the cellphone, Doctor de Roo's phone, it was in the bushes behind his house."

"Good God, Susan, I've had CSI out looking plus divers dredging the river and Rose and you find it just like that? How on earth did you do it?"

"Oh, it's a long story involving throwing stones, I'll tell you over some drinks sometime."

"Yes, but right now I need to go; I want to be with Constable Ryan when she is admitted. Look, hold on to the phone and I'll pick it up later when I get back to Bayfield."

"Okay, will do, but Rose has it right now, better to get it back from her. See you, John."

Susan headed over to Rose and said, "I told John, that we found the phone and he's going to pick it up from you later when he gets back from seeing Constable Ryan admitted. "

"Did you mention that we had unlocked the password?"

"No, I didn't have time, besides, that woman, Deb was hovering next to John, and I didn't want to say too much."

"She overheard your conversation? She must realize that when the police see her text messages, she will be high up on their list of suspects. What do you think, Susan? Do you think she's our murderer?"

"You know something, Rose, there will be DNA on the murder weapon and that will be the conclusive evidence required to clinch the case. Maybe when you see John later you can ask him if they have the DNA results back yet."

FORTY-FIVE

They had reached the Harbour Court Condo's and Rose pulled up into the car park to let Susan out.

She waved to her friend and turned the car around and drove back across the river to Bayfield Terrace. Getting out of her car, Rose suddenly felt a wave of exhaustion wash over her plus the fact that her stomach was grumbling. She and Susan had not had lunch and now she was absolutely starving.

Ben and Puff ran to the door barking with delight and Tom came to the door to give Rose a big kiss, the smell of curry cooking wafted her way.

"I'm cooking dinner tonight, love." Tom said with a big grin on his face.

"Good, I'm starving. I'm going to have a little something to tide me over though, Tom. I skipped out on lunch and am ravenous now."

"You go and sit in the sunroom, and I'll bring you some cheese and biscuits. Oh, by the way, Kate's on her way round;

I'll pour out two glasses of wine for you girls and leave you both to chat."

"Thank you, darling." Rose said and proceeded to walk through to the sunroom followed by the two dogs.

Ten minutes later there was a knock on the door and Kate appeared looking a little flustered. It was five o'clock.

"Rose, I just heard from John, we were supposed to be having dinner tonight at The Little Inn but he's not sure if he'll be back in time. God, poor Constable Ryan, he told me about it and that you were there too. Honestly, Rose, you could have been killed."

"Hardly, I was in our car parked a kilometre away and I actually missed all the action. Although, I believe there was quiet a commotion."

Just then Tom entered the sunroom carrying a tray with two glasses of wine and a plate of cheese and biscuits.

"Here you both are. Now, I'm going to take the dogs for a quick walk before I put the rice on. Kate, do you want to stay for dinner?"

"Oh, Tom, I'm not sure if my dinner date with John is on or off. He's at Clinton Hospital right now waiting for the doctors to release some information about Constable Ryan's condition. I'll have some of this cheese though and hope that my dinner with John is not cancelled. Hopefully, we'll just have a later than planned meal."

"Okay, see you both later, come on Puff and Ben." Tom waved their leashes in the air and they both got up with wagging tails and trotted over to where he stood.

Rose and Kate sat and chatted amicably, and Kate was just about to leave when there was a knock on the door. Without the dogs around to bark, at first Rose didn't hear the knock. She finally got up and went to the front door. To her astonishment,

Doctor Deb Cave was standing on the doorstep. Rose was quite taken back, but invited her in.

"Doctor Cave, I thought that after your ordeal you'd be safely back in London, how can I help you?"

Deb stepped into the hallway and looked around Rose and Tom's house. Kate, hearing the voices, ambled into the hall.

"Oh, hi. I'm Kate, Rose's sister."

"Kate, this is Doctor Cave. She was the research assistant to poor Doctor de Roo. John was shut in the shed with her, and they managed to escape together just in time to witness poor Constable Ryan being shot."

Kate's eyes had grown large with alarm.

"Gosh, you poor thing, what a trauma for you and John, are you sure that you're okay? Would you like a glass of wine?"

Rose looked at her sister with amazement, she wanted to kick her. How dare she invite Doctor Cave in for a glass of wine? She, however, didn't say a word and just ushered Deb into the sunroom.

"I'll just get another glass and grab the bottle of wine. You two go ahead, I'll be back in a minute."

Rose slipped into the kitchen and reached for her cellphone. She sent a quick message to John asking for his immediate help. She knew that the message would sound cryptic but knowing John he would respond as soon as he could. Rose wasn't sure if she could handle Doctor Cave on her own.

Returning to the sunroom she found Kate and Dr. Cave in deep conversation. They were talking about the dump found on the Wilson property and how, over the years, PCBs had leeched into the groundwater. Kate looked suitably horrified and appeared to be hanging on Deb's every word.

"So this man, Steve, has he been arrested? Did he murder Doctor de Roo?"

Rose held her breath and waited to hear Deb's reply. It was terrible knowing what she knew about the relationship between the two doctors, she felt like a spy. Biting her lip and listening to Deb's answer, she held her breath.

"I should imagine that the police will find that he's their man as who else would have wanted him silenced?"

"It strikes me as a bit drastic killing a man over a dump of all things, even though it is a toxic one at that." Kate said in a flippant tone of voice.

Deb answered quickly, "Well, the Ministry will fine him possibly a million dollars penalty plus the clean up costs. That is a good enough reason to want to keep the location of the dump secret I would have thought. Anyway, who else would want him out of the way?"

Who else indeed, thought Rose.

"So, Doctor Cave, how exactly can I help you? I presume that you came to visit me for a reason?"

Deb stood up abruptly and suddenly her whole demeanour became more serious.

"Yes, well, I believe that you found Hendrich's cellphone? I need that phone. You have to hand it over to me now."

Rose looked at her with astonishment. How dare she so brazenly come into her house and demand the phone just like that? Did she truly expect her to just hand it over to her willingly without questioning why?

Kate now also looked at Doctor Cave quizzically, there was obviously something going on here of which she was unaware.

It suddenly dawned on her that she was the one to have invited this strange and demanding woman to join them in a glass of wine. Kate got up and slowly picked up the wine glasses and plate of cheese and put them on the tray. She walked into the kitchen leaving Rose and Doctor Cave at a standstill. The next thing that happened seemed unreal to Kate. One minute she was standing in the kitchen uncertain whether or not she should try and rescue her sister from Doctor Cave and if so, how would she succeed to politely tell the woman to leave, when Deb came rushing into the kitchen, grabbed one of the knives from the rack, and before Kate could shout out to Rose, she felt the cold steel of a knife pressed against her throat and Deb's arms tightly wound around her body. Rose appeared in the kitchen and gasped.

"What on earth are you doing? Let my sister go this minute."

"Not until you give me the phone." Deb growled and tightened her grip on Kate.

Rose stood there, undecided what to do next.

FORTY-SIX

John left Clinton hospital having seen Holly comfortably settled in a private bed in a quiet ward. She had come through surgery successfully and was now recuperating. Her shoulder would always bare the scar of where the bullet had been removed but the doctors were confident that she would make a speedy recovery. As her fiancé had arrived, John took his leave.

Driving back to Bayfield John decided to make a small detour to visit the OPP detachment on Highway 21, he wanted to have a preliminary interview with Steve Wilson. In all likelihood the man would have to be arraigned in London, but he wasn't himself a hundred percent sure that he was their man for the murder of Doctor de Roo.

Pulling into the station he checked in at the reception desk. The sergeant in charge told him to wait in the interview room, he would bring Steve up from the basement cells.

John looked at his watch, it was already five-thirty. he would be late for his dinner date with Kate. He reached for his phone and sent her a rather garbled text message the gist of it being that he would call her when he got back to Bayfield, with that accomplished, he waited patiently for Steve Wilson.

When they finally brought him into the interview room, instead of seeing the bombastic, aggressive man they had witnessed out on Parr Line, a frightened, passive person stood before him. His will had been broken like a wild stallion. John smiled as this was going to be much easier than he thought.

"Take a seat." John said gruffly, "I probably don't need to read you your Miranda rights, but just be aware that anything that you say or do may be held against you in a court of law. Now, Steve, where were you last Thursday?"

Steve looked mulish and for one moment John thought he was going to have to deal with his pig headedness, but then he answered in a resigned voice.

"Thursday morning I was at the Happy Valley Adult Community Park outside Bayfield. I'm the parks maintenance guy. I think that I was cleaning gutters that day if I remember rightly."

"Did you ever go down to Doctor de Roo's house by the river?"

"Not really. Oh, I sometimes take garden waste like leaves, branches, and logs down in a wheelbarrow and make a pile by the river, why do you ask?"

"You do know that Doctor de Roo was murdered right down by the river outside his house. His body was found down by the river flats near the new bridge construction."

"Surely you cannot think that I had anything to do with that, do you?" Steve looked alarmed.

"We most certainly have you marked down as a definite person of interest. Whether you are up for a murder charge or not has yet to be decided, but you will most definitely be charged with shooting an officer and obstructing the line of duty."

Steve blanched visibly at the mention of the charge against him, but he blustered on. "I cannot, and will not, deny shooting your officer, but I will totally deny anything to do with the murder. Hell, I never even knew the man. Why would I want to kill someone I didn't know?"

"Did you not know that his assistant, Doctor Cave and he were about to reveal that you had a potentially toxic dump on your property, one that had leeched into the ground water system and into the river?"

Steve looked perplexed. "The first that I heard of this was yesterday when that stuck-up bitch, Doctor something, told me that the Ministry of the Environment would be onto me for having the dump. You realize something, that heap of metal has been in the woods as long as I can remember, and I never questioned my father about it or indeed anyone for that matter."

"So you mean to say you were unaware that the dump was potentially lethal?"

"Why would I think that? Most people see discarded junk and don't automatically think that it's toxic, do they? It was an eyesore, yes, but what was I supposed to do with it? My father deposited it there, not me."

"Well, it's not my job to judge, but you own the property now, so I suppose you've inherited the clean up too. Are you sure you never had any contact with either Doctor de Roo or Doctor Cave prior to yesterday?"

"I swear, now go ahead and charge me and leave me in peace."

John realized that there was no point going on; the man had clammed up and he knew that he'd get no more out of him.

He stood up and indicated to the officer in charge that he was ready to go.

Before leaving the station John took out his phone to call Kate. It was then that he noticed Rose's text.

HELP ME

Oh my God, he thought, *not Rose*. He jumped into his car and drove like a bat out of hell to Bayfield with his heart in his throat.

FORTY-SEVEN

Tom opened the front door, and the dogs went charging in. He called out to Rose that he was back and as he walked into the kitchen, he stopped dead in his tracks. Doctor Cave had Kate in a bear hug with a knife to her throat and Rose was standing in the doorway with her mouth open.

Dr. Cave shouted out, "I'm not going to say it again, give me the phone and then I'll leave you in peace. As to you," she turned to look at Tom, "I don't know who you are, but don't get any ideas about being a hero. I swear I'll cut Kate's throat if Rose doesn't give me the phone."

"For God's sake, Rose, give her the blasted phone."

"Oh, alright, but it's in my purse." Rose moved into the hall to reach her purse. She pulled out the phone and held it in the air and before Deb could say anything, she threw it directly at her aiming for her face. Deb flinched as the phone sailed past her just inches away. In that split second, Tom was onto her at the same time as Kate, who let out a mighty kick. Deb buckled over dropping the knife onto the floor. Rose ran to pick it up and Tom knocked Deb to the ground, sitting on top of her. Deb shouted and thrashed around like a mad woman.

It was this scene of utter pandemonium that John found himself witnessing as he burst into the Blair's house. He immediately rushed over to Rose and said, "Thank God, Rose, thank God you're alright." He then pulled the deranged woman off the floor and took out his zip tie hand cuffs.

"I'm having to arrest you, Deb. You have one hell of lot of explaining to do as I haven't a clue what's been going on here. I'm sure that Rose and Tom will enlighten me."

Kate had sunk down onto a kitchen chair, delayed shock had begun to set in, and she started to shake all over. Rose ran over to her sister and wrapped her arms around her.

"You'll be alright, sis, look come into the sunroom and I'll pour you out a stiff brandy. Thank you, Tom," she whispered as she passed him in the hall. She guided Kate into the sunroom and sat her down on the sofa. Puff and Ben jumped up and snuggled next to her.

"Just wait here and I'll be back in a second with your brandy. I must have a quick word with John and Tom. They need to know what this was all about."

Rose quickly went back into the kitchen and signalled to John that she wanted a word.

"Tom, could you watch her for a minute, I've called Sergeant Flowers and he'll be here very soon to take her away."

John walked into the hall and had to stop himself from throwing his arms around Rose. He wanted so much to kiss her and hold her tight against his chest, it physically hurt restraining himself. Rose just stood there, and he just knew that she wanted him as much as he wanted her.

Finally, she let out a deep sigh and said quietly, "John, I think Doctor Cave did it, I think she murdered Hendrich. You need to look at the text messages on the phone. She tried to get the phone off me and took Kate as hostage. Oh, John it was awful." Rose stifled a sob.

"Where is the phone now, Rose?" John said gently.

"I threw it at her. I think that it's on the kitchen floor. We managed to crack the password courtesy of old Bill Burns. The password is 3927. When you read the text messages, you'll understand what I'm on about."

The front door burst open, and Sergeant Flowers rushed in. He stopped immediately when he saw John and Rose deep in conversation.

"She's in the kitchen. Take her away, Sergeant; I'll be there shortly, read her the rights and get the recorder set up. This is one interview that needs to be done by the books."

Kate stood up as Sergeant Flowers entered the room and she walked slowly towards John and Rose.

"Are you alright, Kate?" John asked. "Will you still be up for dinner tonight?"

"I don't think so, John, maybe you could come over later for a drink. We need to talk."

Tom went over to Rose and put his arms around her.

"Are you alright, love?"

"Yes, darling, I'm okay. You were pretty heroic back there."

"I still don't know what just happened, but I'm sure you're going to tell me. I'll put the rice on and maybe you can reveal all to me over the curry."

Rose nodded and looked at her husband, he was such a good man, and she did love him so.

FORTY-EIGHT

John sat opposite Deb Cave down in the basement of the Town Hall and proceeded to issue her the standard Miranda rights.

"Doctor Cave, I have to remind you of your rights, you don't have to say anything, however anything that you do say may be used against you in a court of law. You are entitled to a lawyer if you so please."

Deb sat in silence.

"Right, well, let's get started. Doctor Cave, where were you last Thursday?"

Deb looked defiant, but she answered him bluntly.

"I was at the university teaching. I'm sure that my assistant, Tamara can vouch for me. I'm always in the department from nine until about four. Why do you ask? Surely you cannot think for a minute that I had anything to do with Hendrich's murder?"

John kept his silence, he had long since learnt that keeping quiet often unnerved suspects into talking and then that often lead to admissions of guilt.

"Look, Hendrich and I collaborated in a research paper together, for heavens sake, he was my advisor throughout my doctorate, and he was my mentor and friend. Why would I want him dead?"

Still John kept his silence. He waited patiently for what he knew would finally be blurted out.

"Oh, for God's sake, I loved him, and he loved me, I wanted to share the rest of my life with him."

John eventually opened his mouth to speak.

"Doctor Cave, I have a record of your text messages here in front of me. Sergeant, turn on the SMART Board and let us look at those messages together, it might refresh your memory."

Sergeant Flowers wished that Holly was around as she was their IT expert. He had, however, been tutored well by her as had the whole team, and with a tap of the computer the text messages appeared on the SMART Board. There followed a torrent of dialogue between Deb and Hendrich, the tone of which got more and more aggressive.

"So, Doctor Cave, explain on record about your application for tenureship at the university."

Deb went quiet until John repeated the question.

"Well, I applied for tenureship and asked Doctor de Roo to support my application." She paused.

"Go on, Doctor Cave, continue, what happened? Were you successful in your application?"

"No, I wasn't, and I believe that Doctor de Roo did not support me."

"And how did that make you feel," John asked.

"It made me feel horrible, I had worked so hard at the university, and I deserved to get tenure."

"So why did Doctor de Roo not support you particularly if, as you say, you were in a relationship with the man?"

"He told me that I needed a few more years of experience before he would consider putting my name forward."

"How did that make you feel, Doctor Cave?"

"I told you, it made me feel like shit."

"Okay, now back to your text messages, you say that you were in a relationship with Doctor de Roo? Tell me about it."

Deb's composure started to crack as she sat in front of John and her face began to crumple, big, fat tears started to course down her cheeks.

"I loved him, you know, but he never really loved me. I think that he was incapable of love or really from even showing any affection. God, how I tried to pry open his hard shell as I knew that he could give so much if he only tried. I realized in the end that he was totally married to his research."

There was a pause and John let the silence fill the room until even he began to feel uncomfortable. Finally Deb let out a groan and then began to silently sob, John handed her a tissue and waited.

"Last Wednesday I heard that my application for tenureship had been turned down, I was shocked and upset. When I contacted Hendrich he was dismissive saying that I wasn't yet ready to be tenured. I asked him point blank whether he had supported my application and you know what he did, he just laughed. I remember slamming the phone down and then I sobbed myself to sleep that night.

The next day, Thursday, I decided to go to Bayfield to confront my so-called mentor and friend. I couldn't leave until my lecturing was over which was around three-thirty and then I drove straight over to Hendrich's cottage. I found him down by the river taking samples.

You know something, he barely acknowledged me, which made me feel hurt and angry, so much so that something just snapped inside of me. There was a pile of grass cuttings, branches, and logs on the ground. I just grabbed one of the logs and hit him from behind. I'm afraid once I started, I just couldn't stop, hitting him that is.

"Hendrich was dead and so I pushed his body into the river and threw the log down and left the scene as fast as I could. Everything happened so quickly I was back up to my car ten minutes later and on the road back to London, when it really dawned on me. I had killed a man and not just any man, a genius, a scientist, a mentor, and my friend."

Deb began to sob uncontrollably.

FORTY-NINE

J ohn clicked off the recorder and handed her another tissue before getting up and patting her on the shoulder. The interview was over, Deb had confessed to the murder, he would be able to wrap up the case, write his final report, disband the team, and return to London. He should have felt elated, but somehow this investigation had left him with more questions than answers and it had left John feeling thoroughly depressed.

John sent out a quick message to the rest of the team asking them to come to a meeting for a final debriefing. He also wanted to give them all an update on Constable Ryan's condition. Talking of whom he needed to find out himself how Holly was doing.

Sergeant Flowers had been tasked with the job of driving Deb Cave back to London Serious Crimes Headquarters, leaving John on his own. His head was still whirling from the events of the past few days on top of which his feelings for Rose and Kate were feeling really conflicted.

He needed to clear his head and a walk was the only thing

for it. He decided to stroll down to the beach and take in the sunset before going around to see Kate.

Striding down Main Street he passed several party revellers coming out of the Bayfield Pub and Brewery. The smell of hamburgers cooking made John realize that he had completely missed out on dinner. He could pop in and grab a burger, or he could have dinner at The Little Inn as he had originally planned to do with Kate; he decided on the burger.

As he sat outside on the lovely patio his shoulders began to relax and the stress of the last two days started to leave his body making him feel rather weak. He looked at his watch. It was eight-thirty, he really should get going if he was to make it to Kate's before it got too late.

Swigging back the last of his beer he was about to leave when he noticed a familiar face up at the bar. It was Barry Brown from Santé Industries. He ambled over to the man and said, "Mr. Brown, fancy seeing you here."

Barry turned and immediately recognised DCI Hargreaves,

"So, what brings you up here to this neck of the woods?" John said while wondering what on earth the man was up to.

Barry looked somewhat abashed. "Umm... well, it's like this. Santé Industries has decided after all to conduct some trials using sodium chlorite on test samples. I'm umm.... here to collect water samples from the river and from people's wells. The study is probably going to take two or three years to complete, but it's a start."

"Doctor de Roo would have been so happy to hear that you finally took his research seriously. May I ask what made you change your mind?"

Barry looked awkward. "Well, our pet dog was diagnosed with tick-fever, Lyme disease, and the vet said that there was no cure and there was nothing further that they could do. I remembered Doctor de Roo's miracle-cure and his claim that he could cure most pathogenic diseases, including Lyme which, of course, I had scoffed at the time considering the man to be nothing more than a crack pot.

"I confess to visiting Doctor de Roo the day of his murder to ask him about the miracle-cure. Our children were distraught at the thought of losing their beloved pet and the vet wasn't hopeful at all that he would survive, so this was the last straw so to speak.

"I had to eat humble-pie and apologize profusely to the doctor, but he was gracious and understanding and showed me how to prepare the dosage. I've been feeding Rufus controlled amounts of the sodium chlorite for over a week now and he is almost completely cured of the disease, quite a miracle in fact. Anyhow, after that I persuaded the research team that this might be worth a test-trial and here we are about to proceed."

"Well, best of luck to you. Oh, by the way, we have our killer in custody and I'm about to wrap up the case and return to London."

"Can I buy you a drink, officer?" Barry asked, but John decided that it really was time to go. He walked back up to Charles Street and turned left, walked to Louisa Street and to where Kate lived. Lucy ran to the door and as soon as she saw John, she ran back into the living room and returned with Miffy in her mouth.

"Oh look John, she's brought you Miffy as a present. Come on in, I'll get you a drink."

FIFTY

K ate had changed and appeared less stressed than earlier. John thought that she looked quite lovely in a soft green caftan and a pair of strappy sandals. Her hair had been brushed off her face and she had applied just the smallest amount of pink lipstick.

A fine woman, John thought, but not Rose and he suddenly felt horribly depressed. What was he doing playing with the emotions of two women, sisters at that, whom he cared about deeply? It was time to stop, he thought, time to see sense and move on.

Kate had walked into the sitting room which had candles dotted everywhere and soft music playing in the background. Lucy and the kitten were back on the sofa next to Kate, leaving just the brown leather seat for John.

"What can I get you, John, beer or wine?"

John was undecided. He didn't particularly want to prolong his visit, yet another beer would go down a treat, he asked for a beer and sat there waiting.

Kate handed him the glass and then said with her back to

him, "I saw your reaction, you know John, when you rushed in like a knight in shining armour coming to rescue Rose. It was she you were worried about, not me. What exactly is going on between you two, John? Please tell me you're not having an affair. It would break Tom's heart."

"No, we're not having an affair, I promise you. Your sister is far too principled for that. I cannot deny that I'm madly attracted to Rose, but that does not reflect on my feelings for you. Kate, I want to get to know you and spend some time with you because I believe that we have the beginnings of something special together, don't you feel it too?"

"Well, John, I did think that, but now I'm not so sure. Look, I don't want to play second fiddle to my sister. I know Rose, she'll never leave Tom, but that doesn't mean that she won't still be attracted to you, and I don't know if I can cope with that."

"Yes, I totally understand, so here is what we're going to do, let's just take it nice and slow. I would love you to visit me in London. In fact, I'll even cook for you. Let's make a date and then play it by ear and see where it takes us."

Kate smiled. She really had such a disarming smile John thought. He adored the two dimples on each side of her cheeks.

"I think that's a splendid idea, John. What about this Friday?"

John let out a great sigh of relief. Everything was going to be alright. They would take it slowly and who knew they might just fall completely and utterly head over heals in love.

FIFTY-ONE

The next morning somehow everything seemed lighter, and the team all wore smiling faces even though there was an empty chair where Constable Ryan normally sat. Sergeant Flowers had brought in coffee and Timbits for everyone and there was an air of festivity in the room.

John welcomed his team. "Good morning everyone, and a beautiful one at that, may I say. So first off, I need to reassure you all that Constable Ryan is well and truly on the road to recovery. I believe she tucked into a big breakfast this morning. The doctors reckon that she'll be alright to go home tomorrow, but not to work for at least another week.

Now, for those of you not around yesterday there was a major drama at the Blair's house, a rather unexpected twist to the case which we all thought had been sewn up with Steve Wilson being our man. I had my doubts after I had interviewed him and realized that he probably was not our killer after all. So, let's go to the real perpetrator of the crime, Doctor Cave.

"Apparently Hendrich and she had started a relationship and when she did not get tenure at the university she blamed him for not supporting her and in a fit of rage, she grabbed a log and bashed his head in and...."

Sergeant Flowers interrupted John mid sentence which he hated.

"Yes, Sergeant?" he said impatiently.

"Weren't there two sets of DNA on the log, one male and one female?"

"Yes, you're quite right, Sergeant, but it appears that Steve Wilson in his maintenance capacity for the Happy Valley Park, had collected old branches and logs and had made a pile down by the river where he had intended to burn them. He obviously had handled the same log as Doctor Cave.

"We will be taking samples of DNA from Deb although she has already confessed to the crime. But back to the narrative, when Hendrich was attacked by Deb he had been on the phone attempting to contact none other than Deb herself. She had apparently left dozens of text messages for him none of which he had bothered to answer..."

Sergeant Flowers once again interrupted him. This time John barely concealed his irritation.

"What is it now, Sergeant? I do want to finish up this debriefing sometime this morning."

"But when she turned up at his house that day you know, when we had just been inside, she seemed so genuinely shocked by his murder, nobody could ever have guessed that she knew already and when I interviewed her the same thing, she appeared totally innocent of being aware of his death beforehand."

"And your point is, Sergeant?" John said impatiently.

"Well, I don't really know except for the fact that she had us all totally hoodwinked."

"Yes, well, that is often the way with criminals, isn't it? Anyway, our deceptive Doctor Cave in a wave of anger and before she bashed Hendrich's brains in, grabbed his phone and threw it into the bushes. We were searching for the phone in the river and in his house, but it was Rose Blair and Susan Parker who discovered the phone. It had landed in a tangle of weeds behind the house.

"Now when Deb overheard Susan Parker telling me that they had found the phone, she panicked. You see, the phone contained incriminating evidence with all the text messages she had sent. I read some of them and was shocked at how virulent they were particularly coming from someone who claimed to have loved him.

"Anyhow, she panicked and instead of driving back to London after the shoot out, she went to Tim Horton's to clean up and to grab something to eat and drink and then she turned up at the Blair's house demanding the phone. She proceeded to take Kate, Rose's sister hostage with a knife, but was overpowered by Tom and myself. She is now in custody in London although Sergeant Flowers and I took her statement and ultimate confession, all of which we recorded.

"She will be arraigned and charged with first degree murder. So, there we have it, the case wound up. Any questions?"

The team were very quiet and Sergeant Flowers bit back his questions until he couldn't hold out any longer.

"Sir, what will happen about the contaminated groundwater? I know that Steve Wilson is in custody, and he will be charged with shooting Constable Ryan, but what about the actual contamination? How will that be sorted out?"

"Good question, Sergeant and one that unfortunately I am not at liberty to answer. There will most certainly be an enquiry; the Ministry of the Environment will be involved and probably other agencies, but none of that concerns us. There will be, I'm sure, a huge scandal, a bit like Walkerton, and well water all over Central Huron will no doubt have to be thoroughly tested for PCBs, but there again, that is not our concern, it is the Ministries. So, if there are no further questions, I say that we adjourn to the Albion, lunch is on me."

With that the team took one more fond look around the cosy basement of the Bayfield Town Hall which had been their incident room for the past two weeks and ambled back up into the blazing sunlight.

The murder case was over, it was time to celebrate the successful completion of another job well done.

FIFTY-TWO

I t was a sizzling hot day in July, the sky was without a
single cloud and was a beautiful azure blue. A gentle
breeze blew off the lake, which was as smooth as glass,
perfect for a motor launch, but not so good for a sail. The Drift
boat was tied up on the South side of the marina, Holly and
Gary had booked it several months ago, white ribbons and
balloons had been tied to the helm and a red carpet laid on the
concrete dock. The deck had been polished, the seat covers
cleaned, and everything was ship-shape for the wedding. At
precisely three o'clock a silver Jaguar XK8 approached the
dock and Holly Ryan stepped gracefully out of the car.

She was wearing a long flowing white satin dress cut off
the shoulder with a lace over jacket. Her one arm was in a
sling, but someone had decorated this with flowers woven into
the sling itself. Holly wore her long hair loose and had flowers
tied into braids at the side of her head. She was not wearing
her glasses and had been made up so that she looked stunningly beautiful.

Gary gazed at his bride adoringly as they proceeded to

board the boat. John followed along with the respective families, making ten in total.

The boat took off and motored into the Bayfield River where only just two weeks ago a body had been found murdered. That seemed like a whole lifetime ago, but right now another story was about to be written, a new chapter, the beginning of a lifetime of love...

MURDER AT THE MINE, the next Rose Blair Mystery, is available for purchase HERE!

AUTHOR'S NOTE

While researching for this book I became keenly aware of the importance of our water: not only in the seemingly limitless expanse of our Great Lakes, but the hidden water coursing underneath our fields and forests, groundwater. I became quite alarmed when I read about the hazards to human health of PCB's, not to mention some of the nasty pathogens that can thrive in our untreated river and lake water. The awfulness of Walkerton resulting from contamination by e-coli really struck a chord when I was reading about pathogens, and I know that the testing of well water has been strongly enforced since those dark days. As far as I am aware private water supplies are still not screened for some potential contaminants including PCB's. Our municipal water however has gone through stringent testing and reporting protocols before it reaches our taps, including the testing for PCB's and, of course we have in Ontario several watch dog agencies who regulate and monitor our precious water. Our Ministry of the Environment, the Ontario Clean Water Agency, various regional Source Water Protection committees, the Ministry of Natural Resources, and locally, Blue Bayfield. These groups do a wonderful job of not only screening but also educating the public about valuing our most precious commodity on earth: water.

In my book I mention the RCAF Radar Training school outside of Clinton which was latterly decommissioned and renamed Vanastra. It is true that the school was decommissioned in 1971, but I confess to letting my imagination run wild and created the fictitious contractor, Wilsons, who won the tender to remove all the electrical items from the site and, in consequence, created the leaching of PCBs into the Bayfield River. Even though this is totally fictitious, I am convinced that this could happen and is probably happening somewhere else in the world as you read this. A major problem in our very disposable society is what to do with all of our non-recyclable waste? Large municipal dumps are already overwhelmed and will not take many electrical items for obvious reasons, and then, of course, there is the huge elephant in the room: nuclear waste. So, as you see, I have opened a huge can of worms with questioning the frailty of our groundwater supply.

As in all of my previous books I like to include a few interesting facts that I myself have learnt and one of them was Manitoulin Island being the biggest freshwater island in the world. Philip and I visited Manitoulin for the first-time last fall and fell in love with its serenity. Now I understand the Japanese term, Shirin-Yoku, taking in the forest atmosphere, or forest bathing, as there is an air of relaxation and peacefulness about the island that cannot help but reduce stress.

As to my fictitious pharmaceutical company and the 'miracle-cure,' interestingly I had heard of an expedition of microbiologists who had gone to the Amazon. One of the scientists contracted some nasty disease and was saved by being dosed up with water-purification tablets ingested in controlled amounts. The doctor who came up with the idea afterwards wrote up a paper on his findings but was ridiculed by his fellow peers and named a crackpot.

Finally, the new bridge construction. My husband, being a civil engineer, has been following the progress of construction avidly. He has been openly impressed by the contractor's efficiency in executing the new build over the winter. He wanted me to include in this novel the whole history of the Bayfield Bridges to which I had politely said no. I have tried to include a little knowledge that Tom gets to impart to the Thirsty-Thursdays group, but this is only a fraction of the information I have been given. Incidentally, there really is a Thirsty-Thursdays group and they do meet at The Black Dog.

THE WALKERTON E-COLI OUTBREAK

In May 2000 bacterial contamination by e-coli of the municipal water in the Town of Walkerton resulted in one of the worst public health disasters in Canadian history. Seven people died and over two thousand people became ill.

A public inquiry examined the events leading up to the outbreak which including several physical causes as well as the concurrent lack of corrective action from public utilities operators, the public utilities commissioners, the Ministry of the Environment (MOE), and the Provincial government.

Other contributing factors were noted in the report prepared by the enquiry such as improper practices and systemic fraudulence by the public utility operators, the recent privatization of municipal water testing, the absence of criteria governing quality of testing, and the lack of provision for notification of results to multiple authorities.

The MOE had noted significant concerns some two years before the outbreak; however, no changes resulted because at that time the regulations governing water safety were voluntary guidelines as opposed to legally binding.

It was concluded that budgetary cuts destroyed the checks and balances necessary to ensure the safety of municipal water.

Groundwater Contamination

Over 50% of the population of North America depends on groundwater for drinking water and in many communities groundwater is the only source of water for public consumption as well as irrigation for agriculture. Unfortunately, groundwater is highly susceptible to pollutants. Groundwater contamination occurs when man-made products such as gasoline, oil, road salts and chemicals get into the groundwater and cause it to become unsafe and unfit for human use.

A SNEAK PEEK AT MURDER AT THE MINE!

Roy looked at least ten years younger in death, Tom thought wryly as he slowly walked past the open casket at the funeral home in Zurich. He glanced over to the long line-up of friends and family come to say their final farewell to a man well loved in the community. Tom, himself, hadn't known Roy that long, but in the short time that he had Tom had enjoyed the company of the man who became one of his golfing buddies and fellow "Thirsty-Thursday" acquaintance. Indeed, there were at least eight of the guys who participated in the Thursday afternoon social gathering held at the Black Dog, and hence the name, who were attending Roy's visitation.

Tom caught the eye of George who was about to shake the hand of Roy's wife Eileen in the line-up. George, Roy, and Tom had recently got to know each other quite well and had formed a close friendship. In fact, the day that Roy had died the three men had planned to play golf together and then Roy had fallen down the stairs at the end of Pavilion Road when taking his dog, Pee-Wee, for a walk. He had broken his neck and died instantly. Pee-Wee, his Jack Russell terrier, had run home, his leash still attached to his collar and had howled outside Roy and Eileen's front door until Eileen heard the commotion and went to find her husband. It barely seemed possible, Tom thought, that he would never play golf or drink a pint with his friend Roy ever again. Lost in his sad thoughts Tom never heard Alex come up to him. It was only when he patted Tom on his shoulder that he looked up.

"Oh, Alex, sorry, I was deep in thought. Rum affair, isn't it?"

Alex looked sombre, "Sure is, Tom, sure is. You never know when your cards are up, do you? How old was Roy?"

Tom hadn't known the answer to that question until just ten minutes ago when he had read the obituary posted by the funeral home. Roy had been born in 1949, making him just seventy-two. He was far too young to die.

Rose walked over to Tom and, looking at Alex, she held out her hand in greeting saying, "Hi, I'm Rose, Tom's wife. I don't think that we've met before."

Tom cleared his throat, "Sorry, love, this is Alex, he's a relatively new member of our Thirsty Thursday's group."

Alex smiled as he shook Rose's hand. "Yes, I've only been in the village a few months and already feel as if I belong. It's such a friendly community."

"Have you retired here, Alex, or are you still working?"

Rose never got an answer as George ambled over and interrupted their conversation.

"Alex, Tom, I'd like to have a quick word with you if you don't mind. Oh, I'm sorry, Rose, but it is important."

The three men walked to the other side of the room away from the crowds. Rose glanced at them, but was soon distracted by Jean, George's wife, who had stopped to chat.

"Just what are those men talking about? Have you noticed anything different about Tom, Rose?" Jean asked seriously.

Rose didn't know George's wife very well but she played Mah-jong every Monday at the library and Rose had chatted to her there on and off. Jean seemed to be a pleasant woman, friendly and warm.

"Well, now that you mention it, Tom hasn't been quite himself lately. He's been very preoccupied and self-absorbed."

"Yes, George has been too. I wonder what exactly is going on."

It would be a while before Rose received any answers to Tom's preoccupation. Indeed, as the next tragedy unfolded she wondered if that conversation with Jean was in one way or another a premonition, a foreshadowing of the impending macabre events about to unfold.

On Sunday, June 4th, George went for his usual cycle ride down Orchard Line. It was a beautiful summer's morning with not a single cloud in the sky, just a slight breeze in the air: perfect weather for cycling. Just passed The Berry Farm, with no warning, a large SUV appeared from seemingly nowhere. It accelerated fast and ploughed deliberately into the back of George on his bicycle killing him instantly. There were no witnesses. George died four hours later from massive internal haemorrhaging. The driver of the vehicle was never found, and his death was recorded as an accident. His funeral took place exactly one week after Roy's, giving Rose and Tom much pause for thought.

Tom felt extremely agitated and very nervous. The fact that he had lost two of his closest mates in less than a week, had left him feeling profoundly sad and confused. His last conversation with George and Alex, ironically at their friend Roy's funeral, kept echoing in his thoughts like a stuck record.

George, usually a mild-mannered man, had been quite angry with Alex and his last words to Tom were that he wanted to speak to him in private.

Just that morning Jean had phoned Tom to let him know that George had left an envelope addressed to Tom. He had popped in his car and picked up the letter with some trepidation. On some subconscious level Tom already knew what the contents would be, so it came as no surprise when Tom found a copy of George's shareholders certificate with Section 12 highlighted in yellow. Tom read the small print three times over before letting out a deep heart felt sigh. Under his breath he muttered, "Oh, bugger, bugger, bugger."

Three months ago, George, Roy, Alex, and Tom were in a celebratory mood. All four of them had formed a small consortium of shareholders to invest in a silver mine up north, near Timmins, Ontario. They had all put in equal amounts of money - $200,000 each to be exact. Alex had been the instigator of the consortium, telling the men that their money would be tripled by years end.

None of them had told their wives, indeed they had made a pact that they would not mention the investment to anyone else; it would be their private investment and ultimate profit. Not telling Rose that he had invested a significant portion of their retirement savings had not sat well with Tom. He wasn't one for keeping secrets and it had weighed heavily on him for weeks now that the initial euphoria had worn off.

It had crossed his mind fleetingly as to what would happen to the consortium now that two out of the four investors were no longer around; what would actually happen to the shares? This question was answered by the letter attached to the shareholders certificate marked up by George. According to Section 12, if any shareholder should pass away the other shareholders would automatically inherit their shares so that now Alex and Tom were both fifty percent shareholders of the Silvercorp consortium. In George's letter he had argued that they needed to look into the mine and find out more about Alex. Alarm bells had obviously been ringing in George's ears and Tom began to hear them too. If two of his friends had died, supposedly from accidental deaths, would not his demise make Alex the sole beneficiary of the consortium? This thought kept playing through Tom's mind again and again. Would he be the next to die?

Murder at the Mine, the next Rose Blair Mystery, is available for purchase HERE!

ACKNOWLEDGMENTS

There are, as usual, many people to acknowledge in the writing of this, my eighth Rose Blair Murder Mystery novel.

There are many wonderful people in my life who have listened to me talking about the unfolding plot, murder, and motive for so long that I must apologize for boring the socks off all of you. Thank you for your patience and understanding. I would also like to thank Alison, Rita, and Margo for reading the manuscript and providing their comments.

My darling husband has also had to put up with my preoccupation whilst writing and my general reluctance to do any cooking or indeed housework during this intense month of writing. I love you for always being there for me.

Finally, I would like to thank NaNoWriMo the online writing support group for budding authors, for providing the incentive to get fifty thousand words written in one month. It really has been an endeavour but is also an excellent way to keep me on track.

ALSO BY JUDY KEIGHTLEY

Murder at Bayfield Beach

Murder at the Croquet Club

Murder at Town Hall

Murder at the Marina

Murder at the Little Inn

Murder at the Retreat

Murder at Windmill Lake

Murder at Bayfield River

Murder at the Mine

ABOUT THE AUTHOR

Over the past thirty years Judy has written twenty novellas, various collections of poetry and a number of plays. Judy wrote her first full length novel in 2013 and developed it into a series called the Rose Blair Murder Mysteries all set in the sleepy village of Bayfield on the beautiful shores of Lake Huron in Ontario, Canada.

Judy and her husband reside in Bayfield with their beloved dog Susie and cat Thomas and enjoy visits from their children and grandchildren.

After retiring Judy and her husband took on a new challenge in their lives. Purchasing land on the outskirts of Bayfield they have planted a six acre vineyard and are in the process of designing and building a boutique winery.

Life is beautiful and sweet. I feel so very blessed with all my wonderful family and friends who continually surround me with their love.

FIND OUT MORE!

Find Cozy House Press online to read more great cozy mysteries!

www.cozyhousepress.com

COZY HOUSE PRESS
MAKE A DATE WITH MURDER